mudflowers

mudflowers

a novel

Aley Waterman

RARE
MACHINES

"Realistic Flowers" from *Heliopause* © 2015 by Heather Christle. Published by Wesleyan University Press. Reprinted with permission.

Publisher: Kwame Scott Fraser | Acquiring editor: Julie Mannell | Editor: Russell Smith
Cover designer: Laura Boyle
Cover image: shutterstock.com/anutr tosirikul

Library and Archives Canada Cataloguing in Publication

Title: Mudflowers : a novel / Aley Waterman.
Names: Waterman, Aley, author.
Identifiers: Canadiana (print) 20230151329 | Canadiana (ebook) 20230151361 | ISBN 9781459751521(softcover) | ISBN 9781459751538 (PDF) | ISBN 9781459751545 (EPUB)
Classification: LCC PS8645.A84 M83 2023 | DDC C813/.6—dc23

We acknowledge the support of the Canada Council for the Arts and the Ontario Arts Council for our publishing program. We also acknowledge the financial support of the Government of Ontario, through the Ontario Book Publishing Tax Credit and Ontario Creates, and the Government of Canada.

Care has been taken to trace the ownership of copyright material used in this book. The author and the publisher welcome any information enabling them to rectify any references or credits in subsequent editions.

The publisher is not responsible for websites or their content unless they are owned by the publisher.

Printed and bound in Canada.

Rare Machines, an imprint of Dundurn Press
1382 Queen Street East
Toronto, Ontario, Canada M4L 1C9
dundurn.com, @dundurnpress 𝕏 f ⊚

For my mom and for Lee

At the dollar store I bought
a bouquet of fake flowers
and what could have been
but somehow (incredibly) wasn't
It only cost $2 but still
that did not help
                    I planted
the flowers among actual flowers
b/c what else can you do
I was so happy I could have
torn your head apart

Heather Christle, "Realistic Flowers"

Part One

I WANTED SO BADLY TO LOVE IN A GOOD WAY. I WAS twenty-seven and newly in Toronto and only had a couple of people and only knew a couple of places. At first my loneliness bred a desperation that felt too ugly to share, so I tried to mute it with long walks and hard work cutting glass and simple baking experiments and Pilates. No one wanted to chat on the subway in Toronto, it seemed, and most often if they did, they never wanted to leave it at that. Sometimes at first when I got to the city, it felt like any stranger could produce a halo effect and become amazing. Sometimes I tried to attach to those people and then I hurt them or they hurt me, because it's hard to avoid hurt if there is too much feeling or expectation from the outset. I was a loser, cute and desperate with a young face and a free afternoon, an orbit gathering energy. I don't know. I don't want to give it too much romance. It was just a feeling and I thought it wouldn't go away, but then older people said that that feeling *did* go away, and though it was painful to feel all of that restlessness, there seemed to be a different kind of grief that came with its exit, and once it was gone it was apparently impossible to get back. Pure energy, bright as a wet yolk. I wanted to love in a way that didn't take anything from the people I loved or could love. What I mean is that I didn't want it to be about how (much) they loved me back. I wanted to know, going in, that if I loved someone, I wouldn't try and blame them for the pain that love brought with it. And also, I wanted to know going in that the feeling wouldn't disappear as quickly as it came, and I wanted to stay diligent, and consistent, and kind.

But it all felt sort of impossible because I loved my mom, but she was dead, and I loved Alex, but it was so complicated, loving Alex. And starting off, I had loved my roommate Lionel, or at least I wanted to, because I wanted people, but actually Lionel really bummed me out. And maybe I loved some people back in Newfoundland, too; I mean, of course I did, but it's easy to love anything far away, and I also wanted to love in the present moment. It's embarrassing trying to love people in a city where everyone already has a surplus, a surplus of love and activities. It's even embarrassing to really *think* about people you barely know, to imagine them and what they're doing when they don't tell you. How do people avoid imagining the lives of others? When I met someone who could mean something, my thoughts exploded like a ticker-tape parade, each holey ripped sheet containing something of their past, present, and future raining down, all of which I only had access to in fantasy. At Bambi's, everyone hooked up, and it was fine and casual and they dealt with themselves. City people were so good at hiding their hearts, as if the goal wasn't always to reveal it at some point. And in the streets, people went about their business on Roncy buying groceries to bring back home, pleasant and hanging on to composure and life with grace. And there was nothing particular about my difficulty, my trepidation at spilling over, except sometimes I felt desire for something intangible, felt it so acutely that I thought it might split me open, and I was worried about it, the space that it took up inside of me, the way that it had the ability to light upon other people even if it had nothing to do with them, and I didn't want to freak anyone out.

Why was there such an intensity bordering on ugliness in my desire? It certainly felt that way. One thing is that growing up I was always scared of my mom dying, long before she actually did, long before I had reason to worry. Growing up, I felt a space inside of me that turned itself ugly late at night, or in strange and bereft moments of nothingness. Desire is like fear in that they both take up what hasn't happened yet and let it consume the present. Maybe, then, my desire and my fear got all tangled up over and over late at night, enough times that they became difficult to separate.

As a kid, I became bent on the tragedy of my mother's potential death, the no-good outcome, because, really, the only way that I could avoid my mother's death was through my own death, a possibility that provided me only initial comfort. I never felt suicidal, it wasn't like that, just the idea that I could cheat the worst potential thing of life appealed to me. At first I felt comfort in this easy out, until I really thought about it. On the unspoken hierarchy of suffering, it is less natural to die after your child; you are supposed to die before your child!

I would never be a mother; I didn't think so, anyways. To die before my mother would give her a lifetime of suffering, whereas perhaps her death would give me the same, but that was my burden to bear. She had lived through the death of her own mother — in fact, she had lived through many deaths. And she had made a good go of it despite them all. She had gotten out of bed one day and found a way to carry on. She seldom talked about her own mother, and when she did it was in a healthy way, very much unlike the hellish spiral that stole me away when I thought of her death, even when it was just a thought. It seemed to me that once it happened I would lack the tools normal people seemed to have, that I would become a serial killer, or that I would just disappear into a cloud of pink smoke, or that I would never speak a single word again. I never told her any of these things, because they were intense thoughts that would have brought her misery and discomfort. I wanted to play it cool, didn't want to stress her out in the precious moments, hours, days, months, or years that she had left.

So of course, the fear was also very relevant; one day, I would have to live through it. Not that I envy people who fear their own deaths, but in that case, you don't have to live through the part where fear becomes reality. The worst possible outcome of my easy existence, and there it was, the thing that was supposed to happen, waiting to reveal itself. In outliving my mother, in living through her death, I would not become a hero and it would not give me beauty; there was no glory in it, it was so heartbreakingly ordinary to do, it was the thing expected of me.

My friend Casey, who is a pop star, always said that she had too much anxiety, so much so that it made her eyelids swell and tiny red splotches bloom all over her stomach. She could barely exist through and around her anxiety, and then one day the doctor put her on a medication that took it all away. Whereas before she would go around chain-smoking and hunching over having panic attacks, looking good but barely hanging on, and afraid of anything and everything she had ever said or done or would say or do, after she started to take the medication, Casey became a chill kitten. When people said things like, *Hey Casey!* she would slowly look up at them, blink, nod lightly, and then look away. People found Casey appealing in a new way as this iteration of herself, because it seemed like she didn't need anything. On the medication, she became so relaxed that she barely had a pulse, and all of her worries went away.

After a couple of months, Casey went off the medication. It wasn't worth it, she said, to lose the most consistent part of herself no matter how painful, the part that let her know who she was. Without it, she felt like a shell. Some people count their lucky stars to rid themselves of their darkest, most difficult parts. But in Casey's case, she had to come back to it. She had to come back to the most difficult part of herself.

I had been wondering, What are a person's responsibilities when they move toward or away from the most deeply felt parts of themselves? Did Casey return to her anxiety differently, with a different approach from what she had before, and did this new context improve her life that had so long been eclipsed by one feeling? If you move yourself into a new context, is it possible to be good in the world; is it possible to be truly fair in a way that has to do with other people if you are coming from a place that is new and undiscovered even to you?

These were the types of questions I felt, stumbling out of my own context, when I first met Maggie. Maggie was a poet who I had seen read at a small event in Kensington that I attended with my roommate Lionel my first year in Toronto. Maggie had a beautiful face, beautiful for its ability to convey contradictory emotions like awe and skepticism at once with a simple gesture, and when she read her poetry, which was the nicest stuff I'd ever heard, it sounded like her mouth was full of marbles, all dark and tangled and full, which made me feel quietly vital. She read a poem about a castle and sex and the world lit on fire that first night, moving her hands through the air like it was full of honey, and she let spill the last lines like the honey had gotten into her mouth and she wanted to share it. She wasn't famous, but everyone thought she should be and that she would be.

That night, when Lionel and I walked home, I was buzzing and trying not to imagine her entire life. That's Maggie, said Lionel, sounding tired about it, because she was younger and a better writer than him, but I found her on Instagram that night and followed her, and often later saw her in the Annex having brunch, and we never spoke, but seeing her would change my day, making it impossible for me to exist calmly, and I would have to wait and wait until the feeling passed. Like my fear, my desire was both deeply felt and deeply unknown, and I didn't know what to do with it, didn't know where it would take me once I scratched its surface. And desire was the only thing that could burrow deep enough into me that it distracted me from the sadness, the sadness of my biggest fear having come to light.

The next year, my anxious friend, Casey, hired Maggie to work the door at a bar next to my house, called Less Bar, where I also worked, and suddenly, as if it was the easiest thing in the world, there Maggie stood each weekend night looking some combination of one of the boys from the movie *The Little*

Rascals and Isabella Rossellini. Maggie wore a long white wool coat with loops of fabric that hung down and swooped back up to link back to themselves in a bow, and her hair was short and partly yellow blond, mostly brown black, cut into a long mullet; she had big pond-life blue eyes. She seemed to have a force field around her, the protective and playful kitsch of a professional drag queen, though she wasn't one.

Lionel told me that she lived in a house owned by the old man who runs a poetry printing press, and that other than her the house consisted mostly of young gay academic men in their early twenties. I wanted to understand something in her that made me nostalgic for something I hadn't experienced, homesick for a place I couldn't remember.

I felt too shy at first to introduce myself, though the bar was small and there were usually only one or two people working, plus Maggie on door. The nights she worked with me I didn't talk to her, but each movement I made throughout my shift felt intentional, like I was moving my limbs through honey, too, like she was watching, even though she wasn't. There is something life-giving in moving through the world near someone who you want to be noticed by, even if they don't.

One night, I gathered courage. I drank several shots of tequila and went outside of Less Bar and stood next to Maggie and smoked a cigarette. She was smoking, too, and sighing audibly, releasing little billows of white air like speech bubbles. I was wearing a blazer and had tightened my side-pony for confidence. She cleared her throat like a man and looked past me. I didn't know what to say and my silence made me feel coy, but the feeling of coyness could not have translated because she didn't seem to notice it. I thought of things I could tell Maggie about.

The last thing my mother had given me before she died was a book called *The Secret Language of Birthdays*, a book that holds detailed information about people born on each day. I asked Maggie if she knew what *The Secret Language of Birthdays* book was.

What? she said. Oh, hello, she said then, making her mouth into a little O for a long time at the end of the word.

I told her about the book and how it wasn't astrology, but it was something sort of like that. This one man spent the majority of his life learning about overlapping trends of the personalities of people born on the same day, I told her. He interviewed thousands of people. And then he made this book, his life's work.

When I finished describing the book Maggie stood there in a quiet intensity. I noticed that she had painted her short nails gold with red tips, the red sloppy like blood. She looked at me, boldly switching from eye to eye, trying to figure something out. She was taller than me. People get called out all the time these days, nonconsensual attention, et cetera. I did not look like a bad man, but a big part of me felt like one on the inside, maybe not a bona fide bad man, but someone whose outing as one would come as no surprise. Moon in Vin Diesel, young Laura Linney rising. It sometimes shocked me to look in the mirror and see not a buff, car-stealing sort of dude but, rather, a tiny nonthreatening woman. It wasn't transness, just paranoia that maybe I had a bad man somewhere deep inside of me.

That sounds cool about the book, said Maggie, studying my face. A car swooshed loudly past us, breaking the surface of a street-lit puddle in the road like a low-aimed firework.

I could do yours if you wanted me to, I said.

Do it like how, she asked.

Like, if you told me your birthday. I could read to you about it. It's two pages, but the pages are large and the font is small. It would probably take about ten minutes, I said.

She rolled an *R* like "rrrrrrr." I laughed a lot and wondered about the vibe. Then a light of recognition went on in Maggie's eyes.

Are you trying to flirt with me, she asked.

No, I said. I wasn't sure what I wanted exactly, other than her attention.

Two old women walked past us and offered us some leftover french fries, which we both declined. Maggie retrieved a pot of lip balm from her pocket and opened it without breaking eye contact; I saw in my periphery as she pressed not one but two fingers into the pink gloss and spread them onto her lips, her mouth slightly agape.

Really, she asked, smiling.

I don't know, I said, feeling caught.

You could do mine, she said then, and smiled, showing her cracked front tooth. She looked like a baby shark emulating its mother, half invested in the performance of a new fear tactic and half amused by it.

Okay. When should I do it? When do you want me to do it?

The next time you see me, I want you to do it, said Maggie.

I thought about carrying around *The Secret Language of Birthdays* with me from that point, heavier than a dictionary, pulling my shoulders back with its weight. Could I continue to move through the world carrying *The Secret Language of Birthdays*? Yes. Vin Diesel wouldn't even notice that sort of weight.

Okay, I said. Yeah. Yep. I tried to do the "rrr" thing, but it caught in my throat and I coughed like I was gargling salt.

We stood there quietly for a moment looking at each other, maybe mutually wondering if we had both just added a whole person to our lives, or maybe it was just me wondering that.

After work I went on a late walk, and my heart pattered delicately in my head like a little animal had space in there. I walked up Shaw, past the house with the big obnoxious Greek columns that looked out of place and evoked a confusing tenderness in me. I wanted to give one of the columns a hug.

One of the last things my mother said to me was over the phone. She was making spaghetti, telling me she wanted to see the Hilma af Klint exhibit at the Guggenheim. Mom said that Hilma had had a dream when she was alive that all of her artwork appeared one day in a space shaped like a spiral, moving up and up in a fluid circular motion, which was how the gallery was shaped. In a way she had dreamt her greatness into existence, but according to my mom, Hilma was humble and never expected fame or fortune, exactly.

We were going to make a trip and see it together, meeting there at the gallery, spending two nights, and then returning. She said it was important to seek out beauty, beauty as the sublime, the thing that moves you. After we talked, I remembered wondering whether a person has a better shot at being moved if they are predisposed to its beauty: If you think something is going to move you, then does that give it the avenue to do so? Or does awe require a sense of surprise that can't supersede expectation? Did the gap between intent and perception matter, I wondered, when it came to beauty? In other words, was it how beauty was directed or how it was received that was most important?

I ended up going to the Klint exhibit by myself weeks after
the funeral and was so predisposed to be moved by the art that
once inside I saw an avant garde–looking garbage bin and cried
and cried, unable to proceed toward the upward spiral, and
even after the security guard told me that what I was looking at
was just garbage, I couldn't help how it made me feel.

I walked slowly within my new desire shape, letting it lie
down in the foreground of my mind. I pictured myself taking
Maggie's long hands in mine and pulling her slowly through
an empty, dark auditorium full of stained glass windows and
candles. I stopped and looked at her Instagram, and she had
just uploaded a new selfie, one where her face was backlit by a
blue light, a light too blue to feel like any place in the world.
She was smirking in the photo and looking away from the camera, slightly down. The photo was captioned "get a good time."
I pictured her pulling her hands down over my face, softly
closing my eyes with her fingers.

When I got home, Lionel was there making soup, and Alex
was out. There were no lights on in the small kitchen, and Lionel
had piled many sweaters onto the table for some reason, leaving
no space to sit down and eat. I knew that he was working on his
novel because he had filled his bowl up so close to the brim with
soup that it was almost spilling over, and so he shuffled audibly
from the counter to the kitchen table and laid the bowl down on
a pile of sweaters, his hands shaking. These sorts of activities were
evidence of him taking some sort of drug with a long name that
enabled him to concentrate on his writing for hours at a time.

Lionel put one hand into his tangled curly brown-grey
hair and scratched, squinting at me as if I were an inconvenient stranger who had butted in front of him in line at the
supermarket.

Hi, Lionel, I said.

Can't talk, having a breakthrough about plot, said Lionel, picking up the bowl of soup and clutching it in both hands. I noticed that he didn't have a spoon, but then, the spoons had been disappearing. Perhaps he had a collection of them in his room, tinted red by hardened tomato soup crust. Without having to wash, he could just re-dip the spoon, its crust layer dissolving in and through the heat of the soup. Then, he would finally lick it clean, replacing an old layer with a new one. I poured a glass of water, took some vitamins, ate some crackers from a red box titled "Sociable Crackers," and then put them away and took down a blue box of cookies called "Break Time."

Why do you always buy snacks that tell you what to do, asked Lionel.

I thought you couldn't talk, I said.

It was a rhetorical question.

I don't think that's how —

Shh, said Lionel. I need to think.

Okay, I said, contemplating brushing my teeth and deciding against it. I had read a thing about how it's actually worse to brush your teeth too soon after eating and drinking certain things than to not brush them at all, and so I was always vaguely preoccupied with the logistics of an opportune moment to brush them. I went to my room, untied and removed my black leather heeled boots, kicking them into the corner, and pulled off my jacket and black linen pants, letting an old, grey, moth-eaten T-shirt fall from the place where it was tucked around my waist down to the tops of my thighs. I turned on the lamp with the pink bulb and lit a candle, put an ambient, dreamy NTS radio channel quietly on my laptop, and lay down.

When I got into bed, things got ugly in my mind. The rush of Maggie, the way she had made me feel and after, turned me suddenly lonely. I started thinking about how it would feel to carry all of that energy around and not have any idea of an outcome, not have anywhere to lay it down. It seemed she should be there beside me, speaking and allowing me to speak. A storm in my heart reminded me that people are variables and that there was no way to fast-forward to an understanding of what they meant to each other.

Maybe it would be nice, I thought, if, from the outset of meeting a person, you could just get a glimpse of when someone would mean the most to you — the highest point of love between you and a person, a percentage, so that you could know what you were getting yourself into. You would get one shot, the moment of pure love recorded from the future and sent to you via email, where you could assess it on your laptop, from the safety of your bedroom. Then you would get a follow-up attachment that showed you all of the pain the person would bring you, too. You would push your thumb into the screen and feel the love or the pain for as long as your hand made contact. And when you broke contact, there would be no necessity of recovery, just a decision: *Do I want to love this person? Am I prepared?*

As I lay flat on my back looking up at an empty ceiling, these thoughts came out of a place I had no control over, and even though I didn't want to believe in them, I couldn't fully ignore them either. For even if one's imagined truth is not their real truth, if it becomes, for a while, the reality of one's mind, by some accounts it may as well be the real truth.

It took me hours to fall asleep, and when I did, I had a dream that Maggie was at a party in a small room with a hot tub, and instead of inviting me in, she was just telling me about it, saying, *I'm going to get into the water now.*

Without any continuity, in the next moment of the dream I could see her from underwater. I was in the water, too, watching her lower body sink down into it. There were other people around, her people, her friends. They were whispering to each other, laughing with ease. I was just there, had just shown up, but in showing up I felt like it was *my* party and that it would be better if they left; it would be better if I got to decide what happened next, because it was *my* dream, even though it wasn't my hot tub.

When I woke up I was covered in sweat, and Alex was in bed beside me. He was snoring lightly like a cat and looked pretty and glowing, one hand raised weirdly over his head like he had a question in class. I wanted to wake him to talk about it, but it seemed unkind. The heavy, orange morning light and long shadows from the east sunrise elongated all of the books, the desk, the drawing of a girl kissing a fish framed on the wall. I wanted to fill myself with beauty for Maggie, wanted to force it down my throat like a gash of light as a sign of devotion, a leap of faith. But it all made me feel very ugly, very ugly and strange, like I wanted to go back to the party in the dream, but the door person took one look at me and my bad intentions and turned us both around, saying, *You don't deserve to be at the party anymore, it is too good for you. Go home and leave the small and special corners of the world alone. Leave them to the beautiful ones.*

Alex's mother ran away when he was twelve years old. Alex and I both grew up in Corner Brook, a small mill town on the west coast of Newfoundland that keeps a swan pond at its lowest centre-point, the rest of the town collecting around the pond like a tall bowl, mountainous at its corners. I met him when we were ten and feeding the swans one day; my mom told me that the swans belonged to the Queen. Our moms knew each other from Arriba class, a dance fitness class at the YMCA. They stood talking in their spandex while Alex and I took turns smooshing stale Wonder Bread into different shapes and throwing them into the water, where they would then flatten out and lose their shapes and get eaten by the swans. I liked to think that my food was also the food eaten by the pets of the Queen, because it made me feel royal. Alex was gangly and tall and had giant front teeth when we met. He reminded me of a goofy but handsome bifurcated merman.

Things went on like this for a long time. The swans, the bread, the moms saying hello. Alex's gentleness, his trepidation. He would pick up a pine cone, hand it to me, and say things like, *It's okay if you don't want to keep it, we can leave it here.* We made little bracelets out of dandelions, staining our wrists yellow. I loved to see Alex, and the possibility made me happy to walk around the entire pond with my mother, something that I had previously resisted.

Then one day, his mom, who seemed very fine to me, left Alex and his father; she left the whole town, disappeared with no warning or explanation, except a short note so that no one thought she had gotten kidnapped or anything. And Alex didn't come to school for a while.

When he returned, we started hanging out more regularly, and I noticed that whereas before he had been sort of calm and sweet and cautious, after his mom left he became esoteric and full of energy, and he played a lot of pranks, always reading

Kurt Vonnegut, and pulling his hoodie drawstrings tight to his face, and asking people if his face looked like a butthole, and then when no one understood what he was talking about he would flap his hands in their face, make a loud pigeon noise, and scurry away.

Alex didn't like to talk about his mother leaving and instead wanted to keep his hands busy at all times, so I taught him how to make hemp necklaces. Once he got the basics down, we opened a small hemp necklace business called Necklace Party. We sold our necklaces at two local flower shops and made upwards of sixteen dollars a month. Now and then we would see a stranger walking around West Street wearing one of our pieces and high-five and yell, *Necklace Party!* And we would both feel like celebrities.

Alex's father, Robert Delaney, who was very into astrology, had opened a fortune-telling shop once Alex's mother left and told fortunes from their top-floor apartment on West Valley Road. In the window of Alex's house was a cardboard poster with a woman genie, fluorescent pink–lit, that said, *Get your fortune told for ten dollars, OPEN OPEN.* But then when people went inside, there was no genie woman to be found, and instead Alex's father always said that the ten-dollar day was a different day and that that day it was, in fact, twenty or thirty dollars.

I later wondered if that act, of suggesting the presence of a beautiful and knowing woman once you opened the door, was something that Robert Delaney tied into his practice out of some mangled form of hope, like maybe one day he would open the door and, like the picture promised, she would be in there, the beautiful and mysterious woman, his wife, his one true love. By the time his guests realized that there was no beautiful woman inside, Robert Delaney would have charmed them, cracked a fresh Black Horse, and asked them to take off their shoes, pulled the kitchen chair out for them to sit on. Really, what he was doing was astrology, not fortune-telling, but no one cared about astrology then, and people cared more about their fate in a vague way, cared to have some semblance of control over their lot in life, a reality that moves through trends but remains true regardless of decade or context, it seems.

Alex and Robert's relationship struck me as special. Whereas my father seemed more of a classic paternal character, a man with many tasks and responsibilities that it took a whole lifetime to complete with little room for chit-chat, Alex and Robert seemed more like friends or enemies or brothers. For example, sometimes Alex would ask Robert to make us grilled cheese, and Robert would respond with something like, *You got polio?* Also, Alex and Robert would stay up late talking on school nights, where Robert would explain very complicated concepts about mathematics and astrology and poetry to Alex. Once, Alex found out that Robert had been donating money to the halfway house, and when he asked him about it, Robert told him to mind his own business.

Both Robert and Alex had this special quality: they liked to keep quiet whenever they did something nice for another person, but they liked to do nice things for people more than most people, as long as they didn't get caught. This struck me as the opposite of most people, who lauded their kind acts and hid their ugly ones. Also, Robert Delaney didn't look like a dad — my dad looked like a normal dad, I thought, had a moustache and a tie, but Robert was very large, tall, and lanky, with giant hands and feet and long greasy hair. Robert looked like a big inflatable Alex, and every time Alex or I gave him a piece of jewellery that we made, he would put it on and tie it in a double knot, as in forever, or until it broke. Robert, like Alex, was full of beauty.

Alex and I were each other's best and only real friends for a time, and we existed in a sort of quiet childhood harmony despite the tragedy of his home life, or at least that's how I'd experienced it. In reality, Alex was grappling with remorse, confusion, and stress he couldn't articulate but that slowly moved around in his mind and heart, forcing him to grow up more quickly than I had to. I started to see signs of the change — his lack of new clothing or supplies when a new term of school started, dark rings under his eyes that betrayed a lack of sleep. I don't even know, really, that the change stressed him out in the ways I'm attaching to it now. I don't think he realized the implications of his mom being gone is what I mean but, rather, he existed in some form of ambient distress.

Regardless, the spring and summer of Necklace Party was punctuated by a strange shift when I experienced something that I named the "Big Feeling."

I experienced the Big Feeling for the first time while watching a movie called *Where the Heart Is*. In this movie, a pregnant woman (played by Natalie Portman) lives secretly in a Walmart, and during one scene she goes into labour on the floor of the Walmart after hours, lying on her back and sweating and screaming. A surly librarian man played by James Frain follows her into the Walmart and helps deliver the baby, who she ultimately names Americus, which I thought was a beautiful name for a baby.

While sitting there on the couch watching the labour scene, I felt this impossibly large feeling inside of me, like my body was too much for itself but also deeply wanting of something, some action that I didn't know how to articulate. I excused myself from the couch and went to my room, where I paced around for many hours, wondering what to do with this new Big Feeling, this feeling that seemed to carry so much of life within it, this feeling that made me feel powerful and vital, made me feel like smashing a window or ripping out my hair or yelling loudly at my own reflection in the mirror, filling me with misaligned delight.

Ultimately, I decided something had to be done. There was something scary in the feeling that filled me with fear and a little bit of shame, like how I felt when I preemptively opened the Christmas presents in the closet before Christmas, careful to wrap them back up perfectly. I couldn't tell my family, or possibly anyone besides Alex, but something had to be done. I weighed my options. It seemed the woman in the movie was having a Big Feeling, too, could barely contain it, and so she dealt with it by pushing a smaller version of herself out of her body. So after much deliberation, I peed into a small plastic yellow cup with a happy face on it, leftover from my last birthday party, and hid it behind my bed. This didn't quell the feeling, but it made me feel like I had some control over it, and after hiding the cup I fell into a deep sleep.

In sleep, I dreamt that I was a giant snake filling my mouth with sand in an attempt to burrow my way to the water, down down down.

I woke up full to the brim with anxiety, like I was holding a secret that was bigger than me — it was as if, in the absence of the Big Feeling itself, a fear took over to fill the space left behind. That morning, my mother brought me a banana and a cookie in bed for breakfast, which was usual; she sat at the edge of my bed in an aquamarine terrycloth robe with her dainty olive-toned hand on my foot, and she talked to me with attention and care, watching me eat my breakfast, like nothing at all was wrong, like I wasn't some unworthy criminal hiding a terrible secret. That was when I really started to obsess about my mother's death, like my fear needed to latch itself to something that hadn't yet happened in order to stay alive in my body, despite what my heart wanted.

I told Alex about the Big Feeling and the cup of pee the next day, but I didn't tell anyone else. He said that it sounded bad. I told him it was a very important feeling, and it had the quality of lavender tea under the light: how lavender tea looks both purple and green and looking at it, it's hard to tell which colour it is really, because those colours aren't very much alike, yet the tea somehow appears to be both at once. The Big Feeling was like this, I told Alex: both the worst and best feeling, and clearly very important. Plus, in its absence I felt the need to get it back: it had left me with too much space to fill. I didn't know how I would do it, but it was necessary for me to make Alex feel it, too — the fear it had left me with filled me with a specific loneliness that reminded me of how Alex may have felt given the absence of his mother. Maybe in retrieving it, I thought, I could save us both.

Even though I asked him not to, Alex told his father, Robert Delaney, about my Big Feeling. This was my first experience of betrayal with Alex, and I felt it hot in my chest. It was true that Robert Delaney seemed an extension of Alex, but still, Alex had promised me.

You promised me, I said.

No I didn't, responded Alex. You told me to promise you, but then you went on saying it before I got a chance to promise, and I never did. I didn't want to promise, in case it was something dangerous and I needed to help you out of it.

Alex had admitted to me once that he worried maybe his mother was in a bad situation and that maybe she was being held hostage somewhere, and there was no way he could know for sure. It seemed as if he feared this with the women in his life, and he always made me walk on the inside of the sidewalk.

What did he say, I asked, trying to seem calm about it.

Alex told me that his dad said he knew exactly what the feeling was. And he said he couldn't explain it to Alex, it wouldn't be right, but that Alex would figure it out one day, too, and I would figure it out better, too, more than I had it figured out then. And then Alex told me that he told Robert Delaney about hiding the cup of pee, too, and Robert Delaney said something that I will always remember. He said that basically you have the Big Feeling, and you have the cup of pee, and the cup of pee is there because when people know that they have to hide something that is so big and impossible to contain, it is easier to turn that thing into something within their control, small and out of sight.

The next time I went to Alex's, Robert Delaney was sitting upright in his scruffy brown tweed loveseat in the living room reading a giant book that seemed too old to be something a person might engage with. He didn't bring up the information explicitly, but the tension of his new knowledge electrified the air, and it was then I felt like the Big Feeling that I told Alex about tethered itself to the real world, because it had held the attention of a real adult. When Alex went to the bathroom, Robert gave me a knowing nod, and I felt my cheeks get hot and red, giving me away.

The next time you're looking for a hiding spot, look to the vast interior, he said, cheersing me in the air with his label-peeled beer, though I had no drink in my hand.

There's plenty of space in there, my darling, he went on, winking impersonally. Too much space to know what to do with.

Most days lately, Alex would leave the apartment around lunch and return late at night when I was sleeping. In the evenings, I would often get drunk by myself, thinking that this was a good state to read books in, because it made me looser and thus more open to new ideas. Maybe, if the drinking made me feel especially loose and intelligent, I would drink in the daytime, too, and become an expert on all of life, absorbing each thing in the world with grace and ease and feeling very sexy all the while.

Each night for a couple of weeks, Alex would come home and slip into bed behind me. These days, we had been having sex like this, late at night, as if out of time, with no lights and no eye contact. It was so quietly placed there in such a wordless hour that bringing it up felt rude and forward, like picking lint off of a stranger. So I hadn't tried to talk about it with him, which was maybe why it was happening so often. Our sex was usually jaunty and tender, but these late night encounters held something else; they made me feel like we were both horses, my bed our bale of hay and my room our stable. After silently fucking me, Alex tiptoed out of the room, returned with a warm wet facecloth for me, crept back into bed, and went to sleep with such stealth it felt like he might rob me, which was exciting.

I told Alex about Maggie late at night after one of these encounters while he spooned me, so that we weren't facing each other. It wasn't that I didn't want to see his reaction so much as I didn't want him to feel like I was anticipating his reaction, which was something I knew would stress him out a little bit. He put his hand on my stomach, and I waited until our breathing levelled.

Alex, I asked.

He squeezed my hand in response.

I like this person. I'm not sure if it's friendship or what.

Mmm, he said. That's nice.

Her name is Maggie, she works at Less with me.

Alex breathed audibly into my neck.

She's the one that Lionel told me about, the Instagram one.

Okay, cool, said Alex.

I want to see her.

Right now?

No, but like, soon. I would like to.

That sounds easy enough if you're working together.

I know, it's just. I'm just wondering what you think.

Alex laughed, yawning, then bit my shoulder.

Alex.

Sophie.

Can you come with me, though, to see her at work? I'm shy.

You're not very shy in my experience. I'm really tired. I can come if you want, this weekend, he said, then rolled away from me but without malice. Before doing so, he kissed me on the back of the head with a big sound.

Lionel had given us his drugs, which wasn't something either Alex or I did very often, but Lionel had sworn off any drug that wasn't specifically useful for concentration until he finished a draft of his novel, and I knew he had them lying around. We went into Lionel's room, which was at the far end of the hall from my room, past the kitchen and bathroom. Inside his room, we sat on his unmade bed with navy blue sheets while he rummaged through his drawers. Everything Lionel owned was navy, black, or white, because he was colour-blind, like Mark Zuckerberg. I thought it was nice of Lionel, a sort of surprising little gift. While he looked for the drugs, I scanned Lionel's bedroom, which I didn't spend much time in. Other than very spartan furnishings from the office section of IKEA — a metal lamp, metal desk, and metal wastebasket — and some books in the corner, the main feature of Lionel's room was the fact that his walls were adorned with pages from the book *High Fidelity* taped all over with shiny black electrical tape like something out of a movie about insanity. Lionel was scratching his unruly salt and pepper hair and searching deep in the drawer. It struck me that Lionel was handsome, and I remembered that lots of writer girls thought he was hot and that he was apparently a bit of a problematic guy in the writing community. I didn't know the details; that was just what I had heard.

You're a better writer than Nick Hornby, I said, trying to get on his good side.

I know, said Lionel. But his narrative arcs are solid.

What are you doing exactly, asked Alex.

Excuse me, asked Lionel, defensive.

Just like, I'm wondering about the writing process, seems cool.

Lionel cleared his throat.

I'm just interested in your process, said Alex, unaware of Lionel's defensiveness.

I'm trying to examine the narrative arc in Nick Hornby's books, where there is denouement and things, and apply that to my own book, but with a different plot, of course.

Cool, said Alex. *High Fidelity*?

And a very different tone, obviously, said Lionel.

I knew Alex was about to ask Lionel what his book was about but that Lionel wouldn't want that. Luckily, Lionel found the M and handed it to me.

Thanks, I said quickly.

That will be forty dollars, said Lionel.

Oh, I said.

Cool, said Alex. Can I e-transfer you?

Okay, said Lionel.

Same, I said.

Okay, I guess, said Lionel.

Okay, I said.

I had taken only a little bit of MDMA, but still Alex radiated light walking through the dusty fluorescent aisles of Sam's Convenience, humming "Happy Birthday," and tracing his long fingers along the bags of chips and containers of instant coffee. I hadn't spoken to Maggie, but I knew from Casey that Maggie was working door at a Frankie P. DJ event at Less Bar, and Alex and I were planning to go there from the apartment, but then after doing the Molly I felt like it was a better idea for us to get Maggie a present and then go. My hands felt warm and vibrating, little beehives, and I felt happy and nostalgic, like everything was cozy and anything was possible.

I have a special feeling in my heart about Sam's, this tiny convenience store on Dupont across from the 888 gallery and art space, which was an old green-and-white industrial building where people lived until the year prior, and by then it was mostly used for studio space. Alex had a sublet there first when he moved to Toronto two years ago, and I would bike up to his window, which was an old outward-opening window off the sidewalk, and push the window open with my foot, and then we would sit in the windowsill and drink cider as the sun set hard against our backs, which was the first thing that felt at all like home when I moved to Toronto. Alex's roommates were artists, and they did things like cover the apartment in mannequins with pins through their chests or paint every object grey. One roommate named Jazmine had a giant pet cobra, and she built it a tiny castle out of empty cigarette packets inside of the cobra's glass house.

The apartment itself had more of a studio feel, with few windows and cement floors lowered for drainage. In the day, anyone who lived there had to flip their mattress up against the wall so it didn't look hospitable, in case the inspection people came. Whenever I wanted to hook up with a random new person, Alex and I would go to a different party happening in the building, where I would find myself sitting next to someone or other, listening to them talk about their current project, and then the new person and I would go back to my apartment, where we would hook up or do whatever, and once they were asleep, I would delicately take off their watch and place it at the end of the bed so that it didn't keep me up. It seemed like all of the Toronto art people had watches but maybe ironically, or aesthetically, as they had phones with clocks, too, and never actually seemed to be on time for anything.

In the end, the parties started to get too out of hand, and Alex lost a coffee shop job because he slept in too many times after too many late nights, and everyone had to move out of the building in earnest. Now what I have are a bunch of plastic Timex watches in a drawer, mementos, because no one ever remembered to take theirs with them, and I always forgot to remind them. It was nice to meet people at Alex's old apartment, because everyone looked rich and sexy and had a lot of interesting thoughts, but through meeting people there, I came to understand that all of the cool art kids weren't really rich or successful or unreachable, and actually most of them had three or four side jobs that enabled them to make art, and even the most intimidating-looking people lived in modest apartments in the Annex or Kensington or the Junction, just like Alex and I did. Lots of people flirted with Alex, but he wasn't huge on casual hookups with strangers and other than me had only ever had a couple of girlfriends in university, each one for at least a year. The parties helped to dispel a small-town-Newfoundland inferiority complex, which made me feel like there was some secret impossible world where everyone between the ages of twenty-five and thirty-five was living large, a part of some greater context I would never have access to. I learned that fashion was actually just a form of self-expression and a guise, like when you flirt to distance yourself, and that most of the coyest people I came into contact with secretly felt very vulnerable, setting up a protective shell for themselves, a shell in which to hide their hearts.

In the last year, I rented out space at 888 for my main job, which was creating stained glass mosaics for businesses. The job had started as a one-off for a brewery that I worked at when I first moved there, but over time it revealed itself that many people wanted, say, a giant glass mosaic of Frida Kahlo next to a bottle of tequila for their Mexican restaurant. I had learned the craft from an old woman named Mabel who lived in outport Newfoundland; Mabel had wanted to pass on the skill because she worried that it might die with her, which caused her to give me thousands of dollars in materials and resources to make what I wanted as a teenager and young adult. I really loved it, making glass art, because it slowed my mind like nothing else. You couldn't just zone out because if you did you would get hurt. You had to treat the glass with attention and respect or it would retaliate, which I appreciated. Plus it was beautiful to see the world through it, the world as it was but filtered through something extra, green wiggly lines or opulent confusion.

Unlike in Newfoundland, there was a lot of money in Toronto, and while it felt impossible to really be someone with money, the other people with money provided opportunity for those of us who didn't have it; I had several friends, for example, who ghostwrote autobiographies for old rich men who wanted some sort of legacy to leave behind. Although these jobs didn't make any of us rich, they allowed us to lay a hand on affluence, which was sort of exciting. What I found more exciting, though, was Sam's Convenience, this tiny store that captured the essence of what Toronto feels like, some romantic corner of mystic dirty wonder. In Newfoundland, everyone thinks that if you move to Toronto, you live in a concrete jungle and become a PR person, or you work at the CN Tower or in TV. However, there's no real luxury to living in the west end — spaces are smaller and more expensive, people's apartments are very tiny; instead of eating small plates in an LA-inspired restaurant, most of the time I was eating two-dollar Jamaican patties or six-dollar pho under fluorescent lights. Before finding my tiny apartment — which had no living room — I viewed many similarly priced spots that looked like storage containers or abandoned closets, basements with no windows, exposed pipes.

Sam's was red-lit, a carpeted convenience store with little lime green and hot pink stickers with prices on them and no signs that designated different sections of the store. The back wall had an entire downcast concave mirror, making the whole store feel like a funhouse, and sometimes candies were arranged arbitrarily into little zip-lock baggies and sold dusty, piled on the front counter. You could also get American cigarettes there, and niche treats like exclusively white gummy bears. The front of Sam's was the cover of a Jennifer Castle album called *Pink City*, which also captured this sort of sparkly garbage feeling of being broke in a wildly expensive city. It meant so much to me, like it had lodged itself into my subconscious at just the right low moment when I moved here, and now there was no way to get it out. Whenever I found myself at Sam's, I felt like I was experiencing my past and my future at the same time. There was no way to convey this to the store owner, a Vietnamese man who spoke little English and seemed generally annoyed by how long it took me to pick instant coffee or a brand of American cigarettes.

Alex held out a KitKat Chunky bar to me and said, You could get this for Maggie.

Then he walked, as if on a tightrope, to a sodden cardboard box of key rings and started to attach them all together, which appeared to bother the cashier. I clutched the KitKat Chunky to my chest and felt the vibrancy of its shiny red wrapper emanate through my heart. A beautiful object. Then I put it down — it was better to give her something symbolic, I thought. What did a KitKat Chunky have to say about our connection? Not much, as far as I could tell. I scanned the candy counter with urgency; MDMA had the tendency to make me feel like I always had to be somewhere else, even if I was exactly where I wanted to be.

I bought four sour keys for Maggie and watched the clerk retrieve them from a plastic, transparent house-shaped container that carried the effect of a glass house full of tiny apartments with numbers, each one housing a different type of candy. Keys to a glass house. This made me think about how in cities so many lives are wildly proximate to each other, just divided by a wall here or a door there, but each wall determined some sort of fate, keeping us organized and away from one another. The thought hit me like the deepest truth of life, filling my limbs and making them feel leaden. What if the people who should be most important in life were just separated by a wall, and what if that wall meant that those people never met!

Walking down Ossington toward Less Bar, Alex and I held hands, the drugs feeling like a special secret between us. His eyelids were flickering a bit, but otherwise there was little to suggest that he was high. I noticed that he was eyeing the flowers in people's front gardens, different tulips and sunflowers and other heavy heads I could not name, bobbing and unruly but assigned to little boxes, marking different property and different people. I thought about all of Alex's beauty and the silent contract about flowers, how they're there to be looked at and to exist on their own. And even if you love to see their beauty, you're not supposed to covet them or take them home, because that would keep other people from experiencing them.

Alex stopped and bent over to hold a flower close to his face for a moment, and I wondered if he would pick it, but he did not. I remembered once in Montreal we had been doing just this, walking down the road together, on MDMA, and I spontaneously pulled a sunflower out of the ground and put it in a telephone booth to make him laugh.

But he didn't laugh. Instead he welled up with thick tears for the sunflower, saying over and over, *It's okay, it's okay*, and it broke my heart.

I had looked at the sunflower bent like an old man in the booth, and it filled me with shame. It was one of the only times I had ever seen him cry, and I had caused him to do it, because of my ability to destroy beauty. With this fact, I started to cry, too.

After some discussion, we brought the sunflower back to where I had pulled it from its roots. On the way I dropped it, leaving the yellow leaves dirtied and bent, but I picked it up and we planted it again, both of us crying and high, hoping that it would stand upright when we walked away, neither of us looking back to check.

Alex started to whistle, and I nuzzled my head into his shoulder as we walked. The flowers we walked past were starting to fold over and wilt, early fall kicking in, only the robust, less elegant ones still standing tall. It reminded me of how weird-looking babies usually end up being more attractive than really cute babies, once they become adults. The ones with giant ears or strange wide faces always ended up being supermodels, while the Gerber babies eventually just looked like normal humans. I told Alex this thought about the babies and he agreed.

Many people thought Alex and I were boyfriend and girlfriend when they ran into us, and apparently several people thought maybe I wanted that and he didn't — Lionel had told me this recently in the kitchen, that the general consensus was that people thought I was in love with Alex, which I thought was a sort of sexist interpretation coming from Lionel, that it was just I who had feelings and not Alex at all.

While I loved Alex very deeply, there was very much an element of our dynamic that kept me from falling in love with him in such a way as people talked about. As best friends (who had sex or held hands or shared a bed), there was enough independence between us that certain things did not make me feel bad about myself or upset with him as a result. For example, as friends I indulged in gossip about other people, or asked him to tell me I was cute, or didn't mind taking a selfie in front of him. We went to shows and parties, and I would lightly code switch depending on who I was talking to, something I had learned in my bones from my mother, and something I had no idea how to stop doing — it didn't feel disingenuous but rather attentive, like I could reveal the parts of myself to strangers that would make them feel the most comfortable and keep hidden the opinions and thoughts that would make them feel ill at ease if I didn't really know them.

The thing was, over the years, when Alex and I had been closest in a *romantic* way I had felt my independence dissolve, and with this dissolution I had felt very wrong, turning Alex into a wrong thing as well. It was like I wanted us to be aligned on everything if we were romantically linked, and anything that exposed our differences was a threat to my own sense of identity, whereas as friends, I appreciated his individuality. It's hard to really explain but I have some examples. When we would hang out through the afternoon and hold each other very closely, I would feel something open in me that made me need him to justify these actions. I would start by complimenting his body or assessing him astrologically, pointing out how his moon in Pisces made him such a compassionate person. I would also start to home in on his small actions — when he got up and made me tea, I would watch how he did it, pouring the loose tea into the tiny bag and tying it slowly in a little bow and then dropping it playfully into the teapot. I would notice if he handed me my tea first, or if he left it on the table for me to retrieve. When the compliments just made him blush and change the subject — something they always did when we were just friends — I would feel frustrated as his lover, wanting him to reciprocate. Or, alternatively, when I said something indulgent or silly or mean, like when I told him I thought Lionel was a misogynist, or when I shared gossip about one of our friends cheating on their monogamous partners, or when I asked him if I looked nicer in the blue shirt or the white shirt, I would feel his spirit squirm under his skin, his answer seeming to take him out of himself, reining it in to please me. This made me feel needy and disempowered. In those times, when the well opened up and I wanted him to see me in a certain light, instead I felt hindered, isolated, and, in turn, frustrated with him for just being himself. As his lover, I felt like we had failed each other, each of us refusing to honour something in the other.

While I didn't always feel wrong in my indulgent honesty, I often felt like I was bringing it to the wrong audience with Alex, though in those moments he was the only audience for which that honesty mattered. I found myself often wondering, How is it possible for two people to really be good for each other in romance if it means you are always presenting yourself to an audience of one, and having them do the same, and each action is mirrored back in some way, at all times? This expectation was a normal one of life, and people did it easily all the time, attaching themselves to another person, enduring small rejections and acceptances from another person who they love so much, and acting the same through the inner tumult of such emotional movements.

I had been in relationships. But were any of those people as beautiful as Alex, and did I love them as much? Maybe the amount of love isn't really the right thing to be focusing on. It seemed that with men, there had to be a borderline resentment I needed to feel and address in order to create enough distance to let my desire flourish, like I couldn't really be myself if I fully respected the man watching me and felt his eyes on me so closely that I got lost in how I might seem to him.

With Bobby, the man I had gone out with in Newfoundland for three years and had broken up with four years prior, my longest romantic relationship to date, my desire had been predicated on resentment in some ways, because I could safely feel desire with the armour of distance that resentment generated. The gap between us caused by resentment was also that same erotic gap that created my desire, because it allowed me to feel desire without feeling too self-conscious, a feeling that made me forget myself. The resentment was toward Bobby's ego, which made him expect a certain amount of empathy without really having the wherewithal to exhibit empathy in return. With Bobby, I was always making allowances for his selfishness, which in some ways made him more attractive to me, like a little helpless animal. He was cute and tried to be kind, but he would talk about his musical projects for hours and preach some sort of hippie love thing, free love for all, whereas when that love ever shone the spotlight on the other more than on him, or when its free-flowing nature was not convenient to him at that moment, he would reject it. He was arrogant, didn't understand the patience and care his ego required, and he didn't understand the amount of love and attention I put into giving him pleasure, how when having sex I never zoned out or thought about anything other than his beautiful body pressed against me, filling me up entirely.

Bobby had wanted girlfriends who liked to do activities with him, but he didn't seem to really appreciate any of their fundamental natures — not that he failed to understand the difference between women he dated, just that it didn't seem to matter to him, the differences between us. Bobby was reachable in his unreachability; his ego allowed him to pull in an audience, even though, as far as men are concerned, he was relatively effeminate and soft and gentle, and he enjoyed discussing the philosophical, which was easily mistaken for a deep and compassionate attention to the other. Bobby was accessible and not beautiful in the ways that Alex was beautiful, because Bobby was aware of his beauty, ruthless in feeding it. Alex wasn't a big fan.

At the time I didn't realize something that I came to slowly decipher in the years following. The realization was that I had often avoided this feeling, this feeling of feeling like a *bad man*, and so I had sought out people — men — who suited the role better than I did. The feeling was about power, I knew, and how to use it. I didn't know exactly what the criteria for being a bad man was, but I knew that it had something to do with lacking accountability when faced with the vulnerability of another. What does it mean for you to really show up for someone who is truly flayed in their vulnerability, I wondered. But the other thing was that my resentment surely stemmed from the fact that these men saw me as a girl, a young woman, and some simple interpretation of femininity was their interpretation, easily. I didn't feel so much like a girl as someone trying on the role of girl, and reaping the benefits it had to offer, and trying to avoid the harder parts of it, the pain inside. What I mean is that when I performed cute "girlness" — my wrists daintily catching shadows and light through the window — if a guy that I liked took this to heart and was touched by it, or carried the fact of it into the future, it made me feel like a resentful stranger, like he had seen me dressed as a pumpkin during Halloween and asked me every day thereafter if I would like to be carved into a happy or angry face. I had so much history and context with Alex, and I expected men coming into my life to perceive all of the layers that Alex understood — the irony and the performance and the nuance of a mood — from the outset, and if they couldn't do it, through no real fault of their own, they had a hard time measuring up.

My resentment of Bobby was, in its better moments, generative; I would leave his thankless, beautiful, taut body in his thankless cabin-like house on the edge of St. John's Harbour, and I would go to burrow away and rebuild my own little world, fuelled by the desire to prove to him and myself that I could thrive in his absence, dancing in front of the mirror, jogging for hours, knitting giant scarves, and learning difficult Mozart pieces on the piano. This distance allowed me to reassert independence by way of moving through my resistance to him, resulting in, ideally, my best and most productive self. Then, by the time I ran out of steam (usually between three and four days), I would return to him fully spent, where Bobby and his ego would perform for me as if onstage. He would make soup and walk past me, pouring the soup into his bowl and not offering me any. Then I would sit and watch him eat his soup and think, *What a simple, handsome man*, and we would kiss and everything would feel righted and fine in the world, because the things that he was performing for me were poetically linked to the secret things I had been doing in his absence to catch up, or maybe to generate space that allowed him to catch up. The space between these two catching ups, mine or his, abstracted by subjectivity, was erotic and created desire between us.

This dynamic kept us going for a couple of years, before my mother died. But when she was gone I didn't know if I would continue to have the tools or strength to continuously reposition myself in his absence, and even the thought made me feel ill and sad, the realization that when one stripped our dynamic bare, no amount of real love or care was at its core.

This realization ultimately made me hate him entirely, more than I have ever hated another person, like he had access to the biggest, ugliest secret of my life.

With Alex on the other hand, I ended up feeling like a bad man if things got romantic. I am not sure why I felt like a bad man rather than a bad woman. I felt that I put myself in the way of his beauty to see if I could mess with it so it didn't threaten me to the core so much. It was like gaslighting, or possession, like I had power because he listened to me, he cared a lot, and would try very hard not to hurt me. We both knew what I was doing, poking at his beauty with a blunt knife, which made it all the more humiliating for both of us and I think made us both feel like losers, though he would never say this to me. Instead I would say to Alex, *You're turning me into a loser, you monster!* And he would kiss my hands or draw me a picture of a little bird, which was so lovely it made me want to die. If I were able to face myself through it all, Alex would have remained my boyfriend, as he had been on and off when we were younger — I had to be the one to put up a boundary. I knew he loved me, and I knew he would have endured these discomforts if I really asked that of him; I knew he was devoted to me. Plus, he had a very rich inner world, and it seemed that romance wasn't his primary concern — he never sought it out, and he could only be intimate with people he knew well.

But also, I knew that Alex's romantic self with me was not exactly as it could be, that he would be better with someone who could look at a beautiful flower in a garden without picking it, whereas it always took too much energy for me not to pick the flower, and all of the beauty of my intent died in the energy spent not picking it.

If I had used resentment in the past to distance myself from the men that I desired as a way to reach self-actualization and empowerment, then what sort of armour could I use moving forward if I wanted to feel good and open to love? It was different with women, too — I had always felt drawn to women, but often this lack of armour took something away, as if I didn't know how to be truly intimate and vulnerable without having the shield of resentment that made me feel like a bad man when I used it on other women, as if we weren't on the same side. This tendency filled me with guilt.

In short, the answer to whether or not I wanted to be Alex's girlfriend was no: I took no joy in dragging him along in this way. It did not make either of us happy, and so I didn't want it. Maybe it was possible that some manifestations of love allowed people to grow, but some love is so big it takes up the whole room.

I had first felt covetous with Alex after his mom ran away and after he had gained some confidence with our hemp jewellery business and started to make other friends, and I wanted to show him the Big Feeling but I couldn't figure out how to do it. When he started to seem sort of happy and calm again, I thought, *Hey, he's not allowed to take that positivity elsewhere, because I helped him become that way! It is not fair for him to use this new energy in the world outside of our relationship — I helped it come to be and it is for me!*

I pushed this feeling deep down inside, because I knew that I was wrong and that it was not a fair or good way to be. But I still felt it.

By the time we got to Less Bar, many hot people were milling about out front, smoking joints and vapes, and I was feeling a bit bug-eyed and worried about seeing Maggie. One person, dressed as a bag of potato chips, was making out with a normally dressed person against the front window, and no one else seemed to notice. Maggie wasn't on the door, but I looked inside and saw her standing at the bar.

Do I look good? I asked Alex.

Ya, your aura looks good, he said.

But what about my face?

Ya, it's glowy. I love you.

I love you, too. Is it the drugs, or do you think it's literally glowing?

I don't know but I really appreciate you, said Alex.

I really appreciate you, too.

Can you touch my hair? asked Alex.

Not right now, I have to talk to Maggie, I said.

Okay, said Alex, smiling.

DJ Frankie P. was wearing chain mail and bopping around on the dance floor. Everyone was sweaty, drinking large bottles of water. I saw my friends Sam and Nate standing near the front, flailing around. On my way to Maggie, a cute butch construction worker named Nail grabbed me by the waist and licked my neck. All the nondrinkers had chugged Club-Mate and were overcaffeinated, spinning in circles, as if on speed. I went to the bathroom first and washed my face before going to talk to Maggie. When I looked in the mirror, I thought I looked cute, wearing black silk overalls and a white tank top so that my arms were visible, slightly tanned and with a little flower tattoo like a cartoon and some muscle definition from trying pushups, I thought, but maybe not enough to notice. But my pupils were big, like black marbles. I looked a bit scary, so I tried winking at myself in the mirror and felt a shudder of drug-induced warmth course through my wrists and decided it was fine.

As I came up the stairs and approached Maggie by the bar, I realized something that made me feel very dizzy, like realizing you woke up late for work: she was standing silently against the bar, next to Alex, and they were sharing a beer. She had handed Alex the beer, it seemed, and he took a sip and handed it back, and they were smiling quietly next to each other as if in on some joke. This was something typical of Alex; he knew about Maggie through me, and this proximity — not too close to have to answer questions, but close enough that there is famili-arity — was something that he thrived on.

Hi, Maggie, I said.

Maggie lit up and gave me a big hug, her long arms draped around me like the branches of a beautiful tree.

Sophie has something for you, said Alex, trying to help.

I fished the baggie of sour keys from my pocket and handed them to Maggie, shy by the display of having to do it in front of Alex, and then put my hands back in my pockets.

Ohh, I love these, she said. I'm happy you made it. I didn't know if you were going to come.

Maggie ripped the bag open and started sucking on one of the sour keys. She offered one to Alex, and he declined. Then we all started to talk about the bar, how the owner was this sketchy man who hadn't paid the mortgage on the space yet and how it was possibly going to shut down soon, despite being the only good bar to follow the Holy Oak.

It's fucked up, said Maggie. Like he's this straight white guy who only cares about sports bars, but he hired a cool lesbian to make it cool here, and now the space has formed its identity around the identity politics of marginalized voices, but this guy, like, comes in and dirties the place up with his bros, and they leave the mess for the next bartender, and he doesn't actually care about safety. It's supposed to be this safe and inclusive space, but he won't even pay to get a wheelchair ramp put in front, and there's no security measures for bartenders who work alone late into the night, I don't know.

I liked watching Maggie talk candidly — she was mostly gesturing at Alex, and seeming comfortable. In our interaction she had been so coy and quiet.

I think it's tricky to call something a safe space, I said. Like, what, then are you just supposed to let anyone in? Like what if you let someone in who hated queer people or was racist, because the mandate is to include everyone?

Do they let homeless people in? asked Alex.

This was a question I wanted to ask but it seemed like it might be offensive, so I didn't ask, even though it was something I should have known because I worked there. I mostly worked there on less busy nights.

Maggie laughed. Of course! she said. Like it's fucked up to just be inclusive to young hot people with money. That sort of defeats the point.

Cool, said Alex. If I were homeless I'd come here.

Same, said Maggie, laughing.

Although I had wanted Alex to leave us alone, when he did walk away it felt abrupt, like he was leaving an Alex-shaped hole in the conversation that I didn't really know how to fill. Luckily, Nail walked over and took me and Maggie by the hand.

Wow, said Nail. What do we have here? Maggie's a Scorpio, she said to me. Watch out.

I'm a Pisces, said Maggie.

Whatever, said Nail. What a cute little situation. Look at you two little cuties, said Nail, slurring her words.

Stop, said Maggie, smiling.

Nail ran her hands over her shaved head and looked past Maggie. Nail was wearing a tight black halter top, and she was so sweaty that her collarbones glistened, reflecting the light. She was toned because of the construction work and had beautiful deep green eyes. She was a gossip. In the end, she cartwheeled away from us.

I've been thinking about you, Maggie said to me when Nail left.

What have you been thinking? I asked her.

Oh, just that I wanted to run into you.

Oh yeah, me too, I've been thinking about you a lot.

I thought you were so cute that night, talking to me about the birthday book, she said.

I've been carrying it around with me, I responded. I realized that without trying to, I had put my hand on her shoulder, which was wet with warmth, and had started playing with her hair.

Then she took my hands and we started to dance like kids, laughing. We swayed our arms out and pulled our bodies in close. She grabbed my shoulder and slid her hand along my arm back to my hand. I tried to dip her and dropped her, and we both fell to the floor, but it was okay. People cleared to the sides and watched us take the stage, and once we were in the middle of it all, as the music pulsated deep in the lungs, she closed her eyes and leaned into it, dancing with an animal instinct that reminded me of a blue flame in the wind.

Everything became very sweaty, the strobe light breaking up our movements, so every sight I got of Maggie was like a photograph. We kissed right there in the middle of the room, on display like that. I used the energy of our witnesses to be performative, feeling the protection of their gazes that created a safe distance between us, so that I could kiss Maggie as if I was watching another person do it, making the decision to hold my hand up to her cheek or pull her in by the waist by thinking about what I would want to see if I was watching us. She put her palm flat against my forehead and closed her hand around it. We laughed and glistened with sweat, swaying back and forth like we were new to the world. I felt my heart and the music, and it felt rhythmic but outside of time, Maggie's touch like a warm new lullaby shock.

Back in my apartment, things were too blurry and we moved between each other like show and tell, the soft purple lamp creating shadow puppets of our limbs as I draped my body over hers, catching her eyes for a second, trying to move close to her, trying to make it real, to figure her out, something clinical in the expectation of it. I wondered about Alex; my bedroom door had

no handle, just stained glass I'd put in and a hole where the door-
knob should go. The cat could open it with a paw, so I pushed a
guitar amp in front of it as a barricade and moved back toward
Maggie, and we started laughing, then wrestling, knocking each
other off the bed, four lit candles and a glass of water coming
down with us. The sound of water cooling the wax sobered us,
and we got back up, slowly, and decided just to sleep.

Quickly, Maggie passed out cuddled into my heart's rabbit
rhythm, but I couldn't sleep. I got up for water and saw Alex
tucked under the kitchen table, sleeping next to the cat food, his
feet poking out like the witch in *The Wizard of Oz*. I felt lucky
and afraid to have these two people here, two people who were
so dear to me, both asleep in different rooms, close but separated. I made sure the scratchy wool blanket covered Alex's arms
and for a moment felt maternal, like he was my child. I drank
the glass of water and then went to the bathroom, closed the
door, and smoked a cigarette out the window. I crouched naked
over the sink like a little bird, flicking the ashes into the toilet.
The sun was coming up, an orange-pink blur over the eastern
skyline, the plume of smoke in the bathroom the same shade as
the sky below the sunrise, a vacant grey.

Then I crawled slowly and gently into bed and put my arm
around Maggie's soft waist, her bony hip. She turned into me and
I touched her forehead and felt desire poke at me from the inside,
cold and sharp and lonely, right in the place where fear sits.

When we turned thirteen, I became keenly invested in trying
to get Alex to feel the Big Feeling, no matter how hard it was to
find again, or what we would have to do to get there.

I think this feeling can help you, I said. If we can find it.

Alex had been growing melancholic. We had reached our goals of making five hundred necklaces that summer and juggling the soccer ball on our knees between us one hundred times without it dropping to the ground. These were the goals we had set for ourselves, and they were complete. His mom had left in February, the worst month in Newfoundland, short in days but long for its unrelenting winter snow and offensive wind, and now it was late August, and soon it would be time to go back to school, routine, enforced structure. Time would stretch not less so but differently, flowers closing up. And a long winter. Things felt urgent, like it was almost too late.

The pee had evaporated from the cup that I had hidden behind my bed, leaving shadows of silt along the edges of the cup's inside, staining it, memory residue. I showed Alex the movie *Where the Heart Is* that made me feel so much, and he said that he didn't feel anything during the scene where Natalie Portman's character gave birth to baby Americus. We watched it on VHS in his house while Robert Delaney was out, and I fast-forwarded to the baby part, where Natalie is in the Walmart, freaking out about the situation and ultimately going into labour. When he said it didn't affect him, I tried rewinding, and we watched the movie from the beginning so that I could see if maybe some context would help him understand. When it ended it was getting dark out, and Alex just looked at me with a sorry expression in his eyes and forehead. We made bologna sandwiches for dinner and then I went home.

I tried so many different types of things. I made Alex lie down in the grass and poured warm water all over his arms and legs to see if that would do it, but nothing. I took him deep into the woods, as deep as I could, a few minutes past the swans and off the normal trail of the park, over big rocks, following the stream of water until it got faster and harder, water splashing up in tiny white caps from rocks, feral and dangerous. I told him to put his head down into the water and scream as loudly as he could. He did it. To me the sound came up muffled, a tape recording of a scream if the tape player was hidden under pillows and wool blankets. He choked a bit, then laughed.

Do you feel anything? I asked him.

I feel cold, he responded.

A thing I noticed about Alex at that point, both of us heading into junior high, was that he didn't seem scared of easy stereotypes or judgments of others but, in fact, had a way of taking those judgments and flipping them on their heads, ridding them of their charge. This ability set him apart at that age, where usually kids were confused and randomly directed, like I was. Most of us wanted to learn something new and lean into it with reckless abandon, thinking that in it — whether it was Nirvana or smoking weed or Asimov or kissing — we would find a god. But Alex didn't need to think any one thing was the best and instead liked to discuss the relative natures of two contradictory things alongside one another, their merits and their fallbacks. It was probably because his mom had been a great mom, but then she had left, and so he had to hold both of those realities constantly, and he never seemed really mad at her, even though he definitely missed her all the time.

Once we went into the seventh grade at Presentation Junior High, the schools had amalgamated, and instead of a quaint little French immersion class with low ceilings and library voices, we were thrust into the world of the unknown: a thousand kids, all from different schools, and suddenly we were the youngest. Our junior high was plunked depressingly, as if in a parking lot, on a big plot of cement surrounded by nothing but cars. To get to school, Alex and I walked down into the bowl of the town and then up through a forest trail, pushing the tall thistles aside until those postwar stark castles revealed themselves in all of their scary splendour: two brick buildings, kids smoking along the sides of them, the smell of Axe body spray, our peers making out in their parents' cars, then filtering in through the blue doors like ants. It immediately became apparent in this new land that Alex would be popular, whereas I would not.

As if in a strange sci-fi movie, the first weeks of junior high were about dividing up groups of students into pockets of importance based on some sort of opaque notion of potential, one I assumed had mostly to do with physical attraction paired with an essence, the contours of effortless coolness. The volleyball tryouts determined the hot girls. Mr. Young, a man who got called out eventually, but not for about a decade, clearly picking the sexy children over the less sexy ones, the Samanthas and Ashleys and Tiffanys, girls who got breasts first but were still skinny, had facial symmetry, their arms connecting in a long tight V at the knuckles, pushing their giant racks into their necks at the same upthrust of the volleyball, perfect form. I was in awe of the Tiffanys, too. But could the Tiffanys of my class ardently hold a paradox in their long thin arms, I wondered, and fling it upward with such confidence that it floated perfectly above the net? Were they as beautiful as Alex was?

I was a blunt child overcome with adrenalin, all of the chemicals that prepared my ancestors to run from a bear in the woods, all of those chemicals swimming in a layer under my skin, me giving kids ten fresh pencils when they asked for one, screaming in fright if someone gently touched my shoulder to say hello, challenging teachers to arm wrestling matches. I had all of this energy and no chill. I always got one or two pimples in the middle of my forehead and had long straight ash-blond hair and a spirited ponytail. I was lean and solid but not curvy, like a Mars bar. I wore striped shirts from The Gap and the same pair of khakis and white Converse sneakers. A cute nerd, not cute enough or nerdy enough to really fit anywhere, but not unpopular enough to evade the scrutiny of the popular kids, the volleyball girls and jock guys who let me into their groups as a cautionary tale, a thinly veiled loser. They invited me to things so as to bond over my slight eccentricities — awkward and exaggerated dance moves, my love for *Oliver Twist* and the Ramona series and Alanis Morissette — things that they could point to, relieved, as if to say, *Let's stay over here, let's stay away from that.* I was under examination by the popular kids, close enough that if I went in the complete direction of the geeks, they would make me pay more than the bona fide true geeks, who were in a different world altogether, but far enough away from the popular kids that I felt no real kinship, that they didn't really want to know anything about me if they couldn't use it.

At thirteen, Alex wore one of three T-shirts, their thread-bare quality something that while in elementary school had made him a charity case and now made him attractive and mystical in junior high. One had the Meat Puppets on it, one was a plain blue shirt with holes, and one was an old yellow shirt of his dad's that said "Life is fucking amazing" in a funny cursive black font, a shirt that he had almost gotten suspended for multiple times except Robert had come in to explain that actually the message on the shirt was not one to be punished for. Alex was energetic but not forthcoming about his feelings;

he had boundaries that elevated him above the ruling popular class. He hung out with some of the popular kids when it suited him, but he didn't really seem to care about popularity at all. He was thoughtful and curious, reading Freud and Lorde and hooks and Sontag long before any of us even knew who they were, but he wouldn't really let on to that either.

Mostly, Alex's insight made it so that he saw through the popular kids, including the most popular guy in our grade, Chad Michaels, a kid who looked like a young Philip Seymour Hoffman but lean, looked like the word "hockey," his face scrunchy and pink. Once Alex wore a skirt to school and Chad called Alex a fag, to which Alex responded, *Maybe I am a fag.* The year was 2004. Alex winked at Chad, and everyone just watched in silence to see what Chad would do.

But Chad didn't do anything. He just stood there and everyone watched in awe, witnessing a magical power emanating through Alex, because something that should have, we thought, ostensibly taken the power away from Alex actually *gave* him power, simultaneously taking it from pink Chad in that very moment. It was magic because somehow it felt like Alex's action didn't just save Alex, but it saved the rest of us, too, and even though Chad kept being an asshole, things felt a little different at school after that.

Then one day, Alex saved me, too. There was a little party. Tiffany had invited me, just a few of us. It was early March and I had spent spring break in Mexico with my parents, where I became more generically attractive in the eyes of the popular kids: My skin tanned a deep brown, my hair grew yellower with sun plus Sun-In, marketed bleach. My waist narrowed and defined itself a little more with long swims in the pool, and my eyes grew bluer against the dark sparkle of my cheeks.

Tiffany saw me that Monday; she was athletic and masculine, all of her features huge: big lips, big eyes. She had a deep husky voice and smelly feet, the captain of the volleyball team.

We're, like, going to drink in the woods and have a party, she said. It'll be cool. You should, like, come if you want. You can bring someone or whatever, she said.

I went to the party and brought Alex. Even though it was March, it had been snowing and felt like January. Alex hated it, the popular boys with their basic idioms. *Mistakes were made*, they kept saying, like Bill Clinton, shifting attention away from the fact that maybe they had made them. We drank Budweiser in the woods and then, after shivering against the snowbanks in our thin jeans, went back to Chad Michaels's house, into the basement. The beers had taken effect, and I was dizzy and floating above it all, grateful, alive in someone's life, maybe not mine, that was okay.

We're going to play truth or dare now, said Tiffany, sitting next to me, her big muscular shoulder touching mine. She was wearing a pink tank top though the basement was chilly, the resilient nature of popular girls, heeled sandals in the snow, and I could feel her goosebumps.

I want to start, said Chad. He stood up on the coffee table with unnecessary ceremony, cleared his throat.

One of Chad's boys, Ryan, passed around a flask of Iceberg vodka, and everyone took a sip, pretending it was delicious.

Ladies and gentlemen, Chad said, between hiccups. Let's start the night on a high note. I don't want to, like, single anyone out, so I'm going to use this, uh, bottle.

Chad was clearly drunk, swaying the bottle left to right in his hand, gesturing with it, slamming it down on the coffee table. His parents were upstairs, in their characterless and newly developed home with clean laminate floors and big-screen televisions, but here we were in the basement, a land of carpet and old appliances and camping gear, the leftover furniture, some purgatory between the displayed and the dismissed.

I'm going to make a dare, Chad slurred. And whoever I land on with the bottle hassss to do it, he said. So don't even think about leaving. Whoever I land on, and it doesn't matter who it is, has got to do my dare, or else they're a fucking pussy, he said.

Chad acted pissed at Alex when we showed up, but Alex didn't seem to notice or care and gave Chad a big hug. As we started drinking, I caught Chad smirking at Alex now and then, rolling his eyes. Chad laid his large, sinewy hand on the empty wet bottle of Budweiser, the label half peeled off. Ryan and other Ryan, both nondescript in their Chadness, sat eagerly forward on the couches, watching it spin. Chad looked at Alex, sitting to my right, and spun the bottle with clear purpose, tension you could feel in the air. Six of us held our breath.

As it turned in slow motion, Chad said, Whoever it lands on has to, like, make out with everyone. It doesn't matter who, that's like, uh, part of the deal.

I swallowed and watched Chad's glimpse stop drunkenly and too long on Alex, who I could feel looking at me. In Chad's gaze on Alex I saw a flicker of something, desire or hope, possession, maybe a little bit of love.

The bottle spins our pasts and futures, what will be decided for us by what has already been cast. It lands in the present. It lands on me.

Ryan and Ryan look at me with shit-eating grins. Chad looks disappointed but doesn't miss a beat.

Come here, Sophie, Chad says to me. Come here, you little slut.

I move from Ryan to Ryan to Chad, taking the dare with sportsmanship, wholesome enthusiasm, hopping on their laps like they're mechanical bulls. I know it sounds fucked up, but part of me wants Tiffany to see my athletic agility and respect me for it. I don't mind doing it; it doesn't really have any symbolic meaning for me. I have nothing to compare it to. I picture each of the guys in the womb, emerging from their mothers, making a Big Feeling happen. I try to picture them being good, try to picture them crying. I make eye contact with Tiffany for approval, but her face holds the distant satisfaction of watching a good movie, like I am no longer a person she knows but some story for later. I watch her cast me impersonally into the future, how she will tell her real friends about the whole thing, and a tight knot of fear collects in my stomach, expanding up my spine. Each time I latch my entrepreneurial legs around a boy's torso, he closes his eyes, and at least one other person laughs. Nothing happens. Tiffany declines me and says, *Ew, gross.* It feels less like sex than anything I'd ever thought of before, but it is more like sex than anything I'd done in practice.

When I close my eyes the blood-images below my eyelids spin in circles, flip me over. When I open them I see the blurred complexions of my enemies up close as they stick their tongues into my mouth. Some of the boys pull me in so aggressively that I can feel them hard under me, can feel the anger in it, what they might've done if it had just been us, what they might do, regardless. Chad is particularly violent, pulls my ponytail up and bites my neck, leaving marks that I can feel settling into my skin the second he makes contact, him trying to feel me up and breaking the thin strap of my tank top under my zipped hoodie, which I hate, but fail to resist.

When I get around to Alex, I realize that I've been wrong, maybe not just tonight, maybe my whole life, mistaking every threat for opportunity; it seems suddenly clear that Chad didn't want the bottle to land on me, maybe he wanted it to land on Alex. But either way, the move was strategic — once on me, if I complied I would be cast into the unredeemable land of sluts, tainted in the minds of the people, turning from a person into a symbol. A cautionary tale. I realize that I don't have enough status to come back from this, which I don't understand until I'm in the middle of it, which ... a middle of something like that may as well be the end of it.

I arrive at Alex and dutifully start to splay myself out over his lean frame. He takes my hands, clasps them in his. He looks me in the eye like, *Are you okay?* I nod yes but don't mean it. I look at Alex for a moment, scared that he might hate me now, now that I'd ruined everything. Alex looks at me as sad as an old man looking at the ocean and then kisses me on the mouth with a tenderness that lands in stark opposition to the contact I had just made with three other boys. It's my first real kiss. Then he lifts me by my lower back and lays me out on the couch where he sits, so that the crown of my head is in Tiffany's lap. He leans up and looks at Tiffany, looks her in the eye so she can't escape, so none of us can.

Isn't she beautiful? he says to Tiffany. Isn't she such a beautiful person?

Tiffany looks at me, at Alex. She gets shy, loses courage. Her look becomes less remote; she snaps back in, starts biting at the skin on her fingers with her long pink nails, embarrassed.

I guess, she says.

Tiffany and the Ryans start to giggle, though Chad is completely silent. Alex lays me there, supine, looking into my eyes, searching, him untouchable, touching me innocently and firmly, making me mean something. I wanted to mean it all on my own, but I appreciate him doing it.

I love Sophie, he says then to the room, looking from me to Chad, like a dare. I love her, and she's my girlfriend. And we both agreed to play your stupid little kid game tonight, but don't get any ideas. If you guys are going to be assholes, we don't want to play, he says.

There it is: I'm not his girlfriend, but then for a minute I am — safely, symbolically. He takes my hand and pulls me out of there, holding my coolness and my uncoolness at once, my girlfriendness and also my nongirlfriendness, my sluttiness and also the kid in me that led me there. We put on our winter boots and our thin coats; he zips mine and I zip his. He leads me out of the house, out of the hidden and seemingly out-of-time basement onto the street, where the snow is piled as tall as we are, making everything true. He leans his body against it and holds me close, kisses my forehead.

You're too good for those idiots, he says to me, where I both do and don't believe him. I watch him call City Cabs on his flip phone, the snowflakes landing calmly on his shoulders and nose, melting into reflective little worlds.

I don't want you to feel like you're trapped. People shouldn't have that sort of power. I don't want you to get lost. I don't want you to go, he says.

I realize then that he's speaking to me and his mother, saying the things to me that he wishes he could have said to her to make her stay. When we get in the cab, I see that we are free, that once we closed the door to the house, something new is able to happen. But everyone left in there is stuck, stuck in a way it will take me a decade or so to really comprehend. If I'd gone alone, I may have got stuck, too.

In the cab, I tell Alex that I had felt the Big Feeling again that night when he kissed me and that I had started to understand what it meant.

Me too, he responds. But I don't trust it.

Maggie and I hung out through the fall. My hopes were high at first, my hopes for some romance, away from the world, burrowing inwards. I wanted romance but also the romance of friendship. I took what was given. It was often the same: We would go out in long fancy coats, eat oysters. She would take me to art openings and introduce me to her friends who looked like a slightly older cast of *Euphoria*, and they would kiss my hand. She would come over, and we would spend long evenings talking with such intensity about our lives and the people we knew, somehow developing intimacy and blunting possibility at once. We revealed things of our pasts: lovers, current hangups. She told me she wasn't quite over her ex, a filmmaker guy who lived in Sackville. She was seeing other people the whole time we were together, and spoke of those lovers often, revealing to me the intensity of the connection, an intensity which I felt I lacked the tools to match.

The abruptness of this explanation might make me seem chill and adaptable, but that wasn't really the case. After she first slept over, I wondered if we would integrate ourselves fully and with abandon into each other's lives. The first few times, things were flirty and we played romantic, hooking up if we were drunk enough. But quickly, and without discussion, what first seemed sexy started to become a different kind of intimacy, and though we got into my bed together after a night out, holding each other closely, we always chose conversation over physical intimacy, exhausting ourselves with words until one of us fell asleep.

I don't really know how to be with women, she once said to me, as if I had no stake in the matter. I feel like I can't build a house or do anything for women. I have nothing to offer them, she told me.

You offer me so much, I said to her then, but what did I mean specifically? She seemed almost offended by the statement, like it was uncouth to bring myself into her narrative so starkly, breaking the fourth wall of our performance.

It felt like we couldn't come up for air in all of the talking, explaining ourselves into and out of existence. She would come over and stay for upwards of forty hours, and then she would disappear for days, sometimes weeks, on end. She didn't have a cellphone plan, just an iPod that got messages when hooked up to Wi-Fi, and there was nothing I could do to reel her in between those long durations of absence, as if each time enough space had occurred between us to start it over again, like the romantic aspect of our union was a set of Russian dolls, one opening up to reveal one near-identical, at once closer to the core but also smaller, with less capacity. I spent nights unable to sleep in my room, my desire and my grief tangling together, and for whatever reason, when I knew I didn't have access to Maggie, I also felt the acute pain of not being able to reach my mom, not then or ever again. Alex recognized it and held me close in those times where I tried to seem fun but cried late into the night. I knew it wasn't Maggie's fault. It wasn't just her remoteness, but it was disappointing and exhausting, wanting the things I didn't have access to, and I was incapable of complete compartmentalization, a strict divide between the two problems, the problem of my mom and the problem of Maggie.

But as much as Maggie seemed to be going away, in small ways and often, she didn't go away, and she kept showing up, parched yellow tulips between her teeth that she would poke down deep into the pocket of my doubt and sadness, growing something strange but new each time.

For the first couple of months that I spent knowing Maggie, Alex was around a lot. He had found a place to live for December and was spending less and less time at my apartment, but we still shared a bed when Maggie wasn't around, and I invited him out with us sometimes. I didn't tell Maggie that we were sleeping together really, because we had mostly stopped, and it was so involved, trying to summarize my history with him; I didn't want to cheapen it. And it quickly became clear to me that Maggie had many lovers, and our connection wasn't even necessarily sexual; we had tried but the chemistry wasn't really there the ways we had talked about having it with other lovers, though it was romantic at times. Once I realized this, a few weeks into it, I decided there was no real harm in continuing to sleep with Alex occasionally. I realized this one night after I hadn't heard from Maggie in about a week, when Alex and I watched *The King* on my bed. Despite all of the war and mud, the movie was quite sexy. We drank a bottle of wine, and I didn't feel sleepy when it was over. I realized I was leaning on Alex's shoulder, and I started touching his chest over his shirt, feeling his nipples get hard under my fingers. We barely kissed. He just held me close and pressed his mouth against my neck as he pushed himself into

me. It was cute, it was fine; I was sad and lonely in the world
and it was nice to be held close in that way.

Maggie was intensely there and then intensely gone, each
time a sort of whiplash, starkly planting me in two places at
once: the place of our togetherness, and the place of our nonto-
getherness. When I thought about her, it made me sad to feel
vulnerable to someone who I couldn't really reach. It wasn't
like with Bobby; I wasn't fuelled by resentment of Maggie, and
if I ever was, it was just the resentment of not having enough
access, and not of her personality. It's hard not to feel lonely when you're hoping and wishing for an intimacy that cannot arrive. She once showed me a tattoo on her arm that said
Maybe, and when I asked her about maybes, she said she was
full of them. And Maggie's beauty was specific and difficult
to understand. For example, she secretly gave her dad half of
every paycheque. I only found out because one night we were
drunk at McDonald's and some woman stole her wallet from
the table. She chased the woman down a back alley off Bloor
and Ossington.

Hey, that's my wallet! Come back! she yelled, with no real
hint of anger in her voice.

I followed her and the thief, worried that Maggie might
get hurt. There was a dead end lit by a street lamp in the alley,
fenced in by someone's backyard, revealing a woman of about
thirty in a hoodie with little plastic pink beads hanging from
the strings of the hood.

Look, said Maggie to the hoodie woman, pointing at her
own mouth, her cracked tooth. I'm broke, too. I can't afford to
fix this, she said, reaching her hand out, palm facing upward.

You can keep the cash but give me the fucking wallet back.
I give my dad and my brother half my pay. I don't have money.

The woman conceded, revealing a face that had been shadowed by the sides of her hoodie as one that looked alarmed and bright.

Well, can I have a cigarette, she asked.

Fuck off, said Maggie, and gave her two. The woman swore at us and walked away, the interaction carrying as much tenderness and aggression as a birth.

Is that true, about your dad and brother? I asked her. I had complained occasionally about my dad, his new girlfriend, their boomer-specific lack of consideration. She had only said nice things about her own father.

She pushed her foot into her other foot and just looked at me with her big pond-life eyes, then rolled them, smiled tightly, and asked me to buy her some McDonald's. I knew it was true about her dad and brother; she didn't have to say it again. The intimacy she had struck with the woman who stole her wallet was different from the one we had — I got to spend real time with her, to listen to her narrate her past in a pizza style, toppings flying everywhere, huge digressions. I got the campy, the performative, the anecdotal, the romantic. Not the raw, not the vulnerable, not something as honest as how she had just spoken to this woman who stole her wallet. This thought made me feel rotten to the core. Still, after this I wondered how much she had been leaving out.

I hadn't thought about it until the McDonald's incident, but something that united Alex and Maggie was money. Though we were all in a similar financial situation at that point on the surface, they hadn't come from any money. It had always been a struggle, whereas I was firmly middle class. Maggie's family moved around dozens of times when she was young, both of her parents academics who had massive debt and couldn't get

tenure. Alex's mother had been a grade school art teacher, but
his father hardly worked, and when she left they barely scraped
by. Maybe when Maggie said she couldn't offer anyone anything, women especially, this was what she meant. Not that she
couldn't build a house, but that she couldn't buy one, couldn't
fathom acquiring the materials.

Sometimes, when my interest in Maggie seemed unrecip-
rocated and I considered leaving her alone, she would surprise me. One weekend, we were scheduled to meet at The
Common, and I went there to meet her. She didn't show
up, and since her phone wasn't really a phone, I waited for
thirty minutes for her to arrive, and when she did not arrive,
I left. My friends Rebecca and Tyrone had just had a baby
girl named Theo, and they lived in Hamilton, and, actually,
they had asked me to come out that weekend, which I had
declined because I wanted to see Maggie. But instead of messaging Maggie to see where she was or whether we should re-
schedule, I decided it was best to stop waiting around for her
all the time and take a breath. I called Rebecca and told her
I would come, and I left my phone in Toronto out of spite,
and I hopped on the train and spent two days in Rebecca and
Tyrone's beautiful house, bopping Theo on my knee, playing
piano, hanging out with them and playing cards into the
night, and hiking up through the beautiful trees in the day,
feeling the restful stillness of a city that didn't always have
something audible happening in the background. I spent two
days with them and returned to Toronto early Sunday even-
ing. When I came in the door of my apartment, all of the

things in my room had been tossed about, and my phone had fifty missed calls, all from different numbers.

After responding to many messages and receiving many worried phone calls, I got to the bottom of what had happened. Maggie had gone to a different Common, and my absence — an uncharacteristic thing to have happen — created a kernel of fear in her, one that grew when she didn't see me present as "online" for twenty-four hours and when I didn't respond to any of her messages. While the fear felt too irrational to act on in the first twenty-four hours, following that she had contacted Alex and Lionel and some other friends, and when no one knew where I was, and no one thought to ask my friends in Hamilton, she started contacting the police and calling hospitals.

I got in touch with her online and told her I was okay and sorry to have caused the concern. While a part of me felt terrible for creating so much drama, another part of me felt a tiny feeling of joy, as if I got to attend my own funeral and find out that I was loved. When I told her that I was home and okay, she stopped responding to my messages, which I took as her being mad at me, once the relief of my safety had worn off.

But instead, I heard the front gate slam shut ten minutes after she stopped messaging me, and it was Maggie outside my apartment, running without a jacket toward the door. She came inside and ran upstairs and took me into her arms and kissed my forehead a hundred times. When I looked into her face after this, I saw something so bare in there and similar to her general expression in a way. While usually she had a campy air of drama on her face, eyebrows raised, disposition cocked for a big cinematic blowout or car chase or fainting spell, now I saw what the expression looked like in real life, the non-mirror-face version. It was essentially the same dramatic face I had seen her hold so often before, but so different from that, because she seemed to have no idea that she was doing it. Like a mother watching her child run out into the street, only to have her face fall apart as her child turned their back, to gather composure once she reached the child and then, safely on the sidewalk, rearrange her face in the exact same way to show her concern. I had seen Maggie's face fall apart the way she always mimicked it doing and understood then that she wasn't ever mocking anyone else, she was only ever really recalling herself.

Maggie and I spent the night together after she found me, and we held hands on my bed, and she showed me a movie she liked called *I-Be Area*, an art film where characters dressed in fluorescent colours move through the world speaking in poetic psychobabble rather than common dialogue, and the movie made me nauseated because it was a sensory overload, and all of the things that she found funny in the movie I found to be incredibly overwhelming, and I sweated and everyone in the movie was talking so quickly, talking around meaning, and she said it was so beautiful to her, the movie, but I didn't have the sort of brain to understand the types of things she found beautiful sometimes, and she covered me in wet towels to calm me down and cool me down, and the sick feeling made me not feel very sexy, and the time didn't really feel sexy anyways, so we cuddled close, and I told her about my mom, and she told me about her estranged brother whom she had been closer to than anyone but who was now homeless and possibly psychotic, and he lived on the streets of Vancouver and had threatened her when she had gone there last summer to try and visit him, and he said he felt like aliens had been implanted into his brain by the president, and he had threatened her a few times, she told me, but she kept going back to make sure he was okay, and I asked why she went back and whether she felt safe doing that, and she said she didn't feel safe, no, but that the beauty of people wasn't easy, and it wasn't easy to navigate. And in the morning we traded clothes and did each other's makeup, and she rubbed lipstick all over both of our cheeks, eyelids, and lips, the same shade, and it actually looked good while on the verge of looking crazy, and before leaving my apartment, she looked at me with big eyes full of wide highways, and she said, I don't trust people easily, but I trust you. And I asked her if she trusted my soul, and she said, There's something in you I really trust, and I don't want you to go away, and I said, I won't go away, and our souls seemed to come so close in that moment, to burrow into the depths of each other, pulling us down with a weight, full, for one reason or another, with happiness and apology.

One week later, Lionel, Alex, Maggie, and I went to 3 Speed, the bar. We sat on the heated back patio and ate mussels and ordered large pitchers of beer and talked. Maggie sat across from me and linked her feet into mine. Alex sat next to her and Lionel to my right. Lionel had just published an article about the harrowing loneliness of straight heterosexual masculinity and was feeling celebratory. We stayed for a long time and got very drunk.

At some point in the night, we started talking about a book we had all read by Mari Ruti called *The Summons of Love*. Lionel had lent it to me and I had lent it to Alex. Maggie had read it on her own. The book talks about how we don't really have control over the people we love, and to try and justify the pathways of desire in some sort of simple, conclusive way disregards the mystery and magic inherent in desire. It was sort of an Esther Perel meets Jacques Lacan synthesis, bridging psychoanalysis with a digestible love-advice column rhetoric.

I think it's sort of affirming, said Maggie, pulling her scarf around her head and ears so that she looked like a baby. When we're adults, we fall in love with people because they remind us of the formative people of our youth, our formative experiences. The new and the familiar blend together, allowing people to reconcile past trauma through present enactment of it, so that they can reclaim intimacy and get back the parts that they lacked in childhood.

People don't like to talk about it, though, said Lionel. It's sort of weird, the Freudian implications. My boss just changed his Instagram handle to @oedipussy, and now he might get fired.

Lionel had been writing copy for a self-cleaning kitty litter box company on the internet for some extra cash, spending some hours a day responding to people on Facebook, Twitter, and Instagram with those large-headed cat emojis. Cats on bicycles, cats wearing chef's hats and making pizza dough, cats smiling and giving a high-five.

He tried to make the argument that he meant pussy like cats, but people were still mad, said Lionel. Like then it just sounds like he wants to eat cats. His one job is to promote this cat product. Anyways, he's sort of old, um.

Alex started laughing really hard and smacked the table. That's amazing, said Alex.

What do you mean about reconciling past trauma? I asked Maggie.

Just that the way we learn to attach to people follows us from childhood into adulthood, and so sometimes we find a familiarity in people who remind us of our families or form-ative people, said Maggie. Or sometimes we have unresolved conflict from childhood and we play it out in our adult life to heal our inner child or whatever.

I looked at Maggie and she cocked her head to the side and smiled with the side of her mouth slightly agape in the way that Alex did. It made me think of something Alex said about melancholy, taking on the affectations of those you love in their absence. I wasn't sure if this was something she always did or if she picked it up from him. I realized something that made me feel odd.

You know what's weird, I said to Maggie and Alex. You guys look alike. Like brother and sister, sort of.

By that point I was so drunk that my vision wobbled, Maggie's head occasionally overlaying Alex's. They really did look a lot alike, both tall and lanky, hair in the eyes. Alex had a longer nose and his teeth were straighter, but they both had piercing blue eyes and pointy eyebrows, angular faces. It was jarring to notice.

You've got a type, I guess, said Lionel.

What does that mean, asked Maggie. I felt my heart beat faster, alert as if I had just jumped into cold water. I had glossed over Alex, cherry-picking aspects of our friendship to explain to her, but I had left most of it out.

Well, Sophie's seeing both of you, so it's just funny, I guess, said Lionel. Funny that you sort of resemble each other. Sometimes I'll see one of you from the side and mistake you for the other.

What the hell, said Maggie.

Oh shit, said Lionel, looking at me.

I was fifty-fifty on whether Lionel bringing this up was actually an accident, or whether he was trying to bring me misery. He looked at me wide-eyed, and I grabbed my hand very tightly with my other hand, pinching the skin of my palm so hard that I almost drew blood.

Alex started drumming his fingers nervously on the table.

I wouldn't say Alex and I are seeing each other, I said to Lionel and to everyone. I felt deeply ashamed; it wasn't that I wanted it to be some big secret, just that it seemed that Maggie had set up a situation between us that enabled me to do whatever I wanted in her absence, and it was a lot to explain about Alex; I felt protective of my feelings for him, like explaining them away to anyone would diminish them. I realized then, though, that this wasn't exactly fair.

Well, what *would* you say, asked Maggie.

I don't know. I really like you, and when I met you I didn't know what sort of thing you wanted this to be, like if it would be romantic and serious or something, and then, I don't know.

I noticed Lionel had continued eating the mussels while I was talking. Maggie looked at Alex and then looked at me, her cheeks pink. She burrowed into me with her icy eyes, waiting.

I guess, Alex and I sleep together sometimes or something. But that's not really the point of the thing, and when I met you I sort of stopped doing that, but then, you're doing that with people. So I don't know, when Alex and I have sex it's almost like an afterthought, I said. Like it just happens sometimes, but it's not the point of everything!

Do you think sex is the point of everything, asked Maggie coldly.

At the same time, Alex said, An afterthought?

I wanted to apologize, but then I would be admitting that I had done something wrong. Mistakes were made. Lionel continued eating the mussels, cracking them at their shell spines like new paperbacks, dropping the shells back into the bucket. Maggie got up and left the table.

Alex was the only one of the group who really loved me so I stayed there a moment. An afterthought, he said again, raising his eyebrows and grinning. C'mon, man, he said in a jokey voice.

That's not what I meant, I said.

It's okay, said Alex. It's fine.

I knew it was fine.

I ran outside and stood next to Maggie, who wouldn't look at me, instead eyeing the red cherry of her cigarette. She was wearing a long black leather coat with a tie belt that hung on the ground on one side, and my instinct was to pick it up and tuck it into the belt loop properly, but I didn't. She stood side-on to me, staring across the street at the amphibian store called Earth Echoes, watching a man who looked like a crocodile carefully lift a snake out of its bright glass box.

Suddenly I felt, in my drunken sanctimony, full of anger. How dare she? How dare she quietly decide the terms of our relationship and then chastise me for doing the same? It didn't feel fair; she was the one pressing the restart button every time we hung out, keeping me at arm's length.

It's really not a big deal with Alex, I said.

Fuck that, she responded, somehow angrier.

Honestly, like, I don't really know what you think but —

You made him sleep under the table at your apartment when I came over? You just threw him away when something shiny and new came along? It's worse that it's not a big deal — if it was then at least it would show that you cared about him! He's so great, she said.

I tried to look directly at Maggie, my eyes fogging over easily, my brain going slowly, fragmenting words. She wasn't mad that I had slept with him — she was mad that I didn't honour it when she came into the picture.

You can't just throw people away or treat them however you want whenever you want, she went on. You can't be close to someone since childhood and then just pawn them off. I trusted you because I felt like you weren't like that. I thought you were some moral fucking compass, because you seem naive in a way but, like, you know how to be good. You can't just throw him away! But I don't …

Maggie trailed off. I almost defended myself, but there was something in her tone that teetered, delicate and sweet, and I couldn't bring myself to. It was the most real she had been with me, but it wasn't really about me; this idea of me throwing Alex away or putting him aside moved something deep in her — it triggered something. I hadn't stopped talking to Alex, obviously. He was right in there! Eating mussels with Lionel. I could have said anything in that moment; I could have told her I was sorry, or really explained things about Alex and how it was okay. I could have told her my mother was the tiniest woman, so tiny that you could put her in your pocket, or I could have told Maggie to go fuck herself for being such a hypocrite. I could have started kissing her with an unprecedented passion, forgetting myself. I could have asked her what was so wrong.

But I didn't do any of those things. They all seemed too scary, like building a house. Instead I was polite, smiled tightly, said she was right, told her I needed to go home, that it was nice to hang, and that I wouldn't put Alex under the table again.

I love Alex, I said.

Well you should show it, she responded.

I just need to sleep, I said, fishing cash out of my wallet for the bill.

Give it to me, she said. I'm not done my drink, I'm going back in. I can pay your bill, she said.

Okay, I said.

Without saying goodbye, she briskly walked back into the bar and I watched her go. I was surprised that she would hang without me, but then why should I be? I could take my intimacy issues and my hierarchy of desire home and put them to bed, and she could have fun there with whoever she wanted.

Biking home, I felt full of doubt — did I really want to be so intimate with Maggie, or was that just something that I thought and felt the most back when she had been a fantasy, an idea in my mind, separate from our lived realities? Why couldn't I get mad at her or explain the words of my true heart? Did I only want to get close to what I couldn't understand?

When I got home, I put on an old blue silk nightie that my mom bought me when I was a teenager, the small white floral decals faded with washes, and crouched on the edge of my bed, ate an apple without washing it. I stayed there for a while, feeling the thin silk cling to my torso with static. I pulled it off my skin and it kept sticking again, gently electric like a good kiss. I put on Mazzy Star and felt my eyes tear up, then felt the water fall with relief onto my cheeks. I breathed in calmly for a while and looked at my phone. Lionel posted a video on Instagram of Alex and Maggie drunk from that very moment — Alex was juggling something (rocks?) sloppily and singing an old sailor song, and Maggie was laughing so hard she could barely breathe, putting her hands out to try and intercept whatever it was he was juggling. It hurt to watch them look so close and engaged. They looked like brother and sister, or something. They looked like something.

A couple of days after 3 Speed, I messaged Maggie to see if she wanted to see me. I wanted to see her right then, set something back on its axis. I wanted to tell Maggie something important, but I wasn't sure what it was. Maybe I wanted to tell her a joke. I wanted everything to be funny between us, so funny that it cut out every piece of distance and made us feel like we had known each other forever.

She asked if I wanted to hang out "next Thursday." This was a heartbreaking suggestion, considering it was Monday, and she didn't mean the coming Thursday but the one after that, as in eleven days later. I said okay, next Thursday sounds good.

I wanted another chance to show her what she meant to me. Whatever it was, I wanted us to see. But how could two people really get close with that little contact? With that little context?

How could they? Maybe they could with the perfect joke or something that captured their essence. Although it felt like I copped out of our conflict the night of 3 Speed, afterward I felt my heart grow full with longing. It was strange to like someone this much despite all of the distance, considering that in the past I had seemed to participate more in a "narcissistic love," which apparently meant that I would love people more in relation to how they made me feel about myself. Lionel told me about this type of love, and I asked him how a person is supposed to know that they're participating in narcissistic love.

Think about the time you've spent together, said Lionel. And then, think about what you remember the most. Do you remember what they said, or do you remember what you said? If you remember mostly what you said, particularly things that made the other person react in a positive way, then it is possible that you engage predominantly in narcissistic love.

I asked Lionel for another example, and he said, Are you more likely to look at the other person's Instagram after you have a date, or to revisit your own Instagram and try and look at it sort of as if you were them, and then you feel anxious or good depending on how that perception feels to you?

I thought about this and how usually after having a date with someone I liked, I would revisit my Instagram and tailor it to their vibe. Sometimes this meant taking out old solipsistic captions and leaving the photos bare, and sometimes it meant adding opaque poetic text to photos that otherwise spoke for themselves. Usually I did this, but with Maggie I didn't pay much mind to my own Instagram and spent hours looking at hers, which was mostly photos of her own face, or alternately something inaccessible to me, like a photo of a gummy bear with the caption "alimony."

It is hard to engage in narcissistic love with someone who only wants to see you once every eleven days so it must not be that, but then I thought, it seems like she's not wavering in her desire to see me generally. Maybe we could see each other once every eleven days for the rest of our lives, and when we were eighty years old, we would hobble into each other's retirement home bedrooms, shakily make tea, kiss on the cheek, and talk and talk. Maybe we would have husbands or wives and keep this arrangement going, still. Or maybe she was punishing me over the Alex thing and creating more distance between us.

❀

One night, a few nights after we made our date plan and several days before we were to meet again, I was feeling very anxious, like something needed to happen with Maggie or else I'd have to try and move some of my energy elsewhere. People say desire is about absence but really, to me it felt more like excess. Facebook's green dot had her marked as online, but she had left me on "read." I couldn't think of anything truly funny to tell her, no matter how much I wanted us to know each other.

So instead I sent her a poem. I had never really written a poem before. In the poem I described us jumping back and forth onto different beds in a hotel room together, and then the poem detailed the line between performance and ease. Ultimately the poem asked if we could find a way to be less careful and more honest with each other and hopefully find a way to be funny together as a result. It also had imagery about turning your hand into a little rose shape, mimicking a closed flower and expanding incrementally.

After I sent the poem I went for a cigarette, and then I came back and reread it. It was the most beautiful poem in the whole world, I thought. Truly a thing of beauty, revealing my whole heart.

Then I got up and made a cup of tea and came back and looked at the Facebook chat: Maggie had received it, which meant that she was probably reading it in that moment.

I took a deep breath and opened the poem again, and something terrible happened: this time when I reread it, it was the ugliest, most horrible poem imaginable! Like in a horror film, the poem had transformed so quickly into such a ghoulish creature, tactless and full of rude and cringe worthy ideas. I exhaled and tried to quickly come to terms with the reality that I had written the world's worst poem.

Then I brought my laptop outside for another cigarette and read the poem a third time. This time, the poem became, maybe, what it was: sincere but rushed, with quick images that lacked depth but pointed toward something of meaning.

Ten minutes after I sent it, Maggie sent me a message saying, Looking forward to our date ;). I wondered if she was mad at me that I had taken the moment outside of 3 Speed to distance myself further rather than as an opportunity to break through to an intimacy we hadn't yet experienced. *No*, I wanted to say. *Listen to the bad poem. Find a way to let me know you, find a way to have known me.*

The day after I sent the poem, I was attempting to make Turkish eggs, holding a hot bowl of yogourt above a boiling pot of water, when my doctor emailed me, telling me that because I had my IUD replaced so recently, I had to check to see if the strings had coiled up inside of me. This email confused me, because I was not a doctor or a nurse. It seemed reckless to me to allow the patient to decide for themselves whether the medicine was working, the implements properly being implemented. She said I just had to reach into myself and make sure I couldn't feel the strings "anywhere reachable," and if I could, then this would possibly be "problematic" and would mean I had to go back in so that they could check and see if everything was working. I didn't like this email, which made me feel like a household appliance. I also didn't know what it meant to be reachable — the subjectivity of the statement made me feel anxious. I called Alex.

Alex, can you come over and check and see if my IUD strings are still in place? I asked once Alex picked up his phone, after eight rings.

Is that some sort of innuendo, asked Alex.

No, I said. I need to see if they've coiled up inside of me or something.

Like a little snake, hisssss hissss, said Alex. I could picture his face wrinkling up into a squish, which made me wrinkle my face, too.

Alex, I said.

I'm sort of busy today, said Alex. I don't know. Like I would do that for you, of course, but I have a bunch of stuff. Can't you do it?

I knew this to be mostly a lie on Alex's part. Partly because he wasn't ever really very busy — rapt, sure, but not busy. And also partly because the 3 Speed incident made things feel off.

Sometimes I feel like if I fell into a well no one would notice, I said.

Of course they would notice, said Alex. I would notice, like a little dog, Sophie. I can come look if you need me to.

No, it's okay, I'll figure it out, I said, and hung up the phone before he had the chance to respond. Then I held my breath and sent Maggie another message:

Hey Maggie :) sorry, I was just wondering if you felt my IUD strings last time we hooked up? Sorry it's sort of a weird question, just my doctor asked me to check and I don't really know how to like, really angle my way in there ...

Maggie wrote back right away: Hmm, I'm not sure. But I'm at a coffee shop doing some work in your neighbourhood, do you want me to come check?

❀

I felt like an underwater creature who had been caught. Not in the mouth or cheek like a common fish, but deep in the body, rendered supine, floating on the surface. Maggie flattened her hand against my abdomen and said, Stay so still you're barely breathing. She crouched on the edge of my bed like a cat gearing up to jump at its shadow, her elbows heavy on the surface of the blanket supporting her arched back. Her socked feet mismatched, one pink-white striped and the other aquamarine-blue, poking over the edge of the mattress. Her eyes ingenuous, full of ordinary kindness.

Dionne Brand has that line, how beauty lives in the past and the future, never in the present. I had recently read her book *Theory*, and it kept echoing back in my mind. I felt like I could feel the closeness of Maggie in that moment, but then maybe it was the power of a preconceived memory, the idea that I would look back and remember this moment, invoking both past and future in one and becoming true through a disavowal of present. I pushed all of the breath out of my stomach and closed my eyes to the room. Two gashes of lightning yellow danced under my eyelids like a screensaver. Maggie opened her mouth in the sound of a yawn, and then she touched me. The first point of contact was a shock, like diving in. Small buck, then acclimation.

You know, she said in the softest voice I've heard her use with me, You were born three weeks after me. That's all. Just think about it.

I tried to exhale around and despite her hand that had snaked its way fully inside of me. It was difficult, like she had a hand tight on my throat. Her arm was still, but I could feel the fingers searching and worried about when she reached the wall in there, whether there would be pain.

Just think about it, she said again. I was only about eight pounds when you were fully emerging from another body. We were being passed around at the same point in time. We probably didn't touch the ground at all for a long while. Both of us were handed into different arms, laid down on surfaces, faced upward. We had the same vantage points.

I thought about us both the sizes of bags of sugar and floating through the air, and I started to cry, the sensation cavernous, a new hidden body of activity inside me that exhausted every other one, lighting upon the fatigue of every other moving part. I broke into sobs and Maggie asked if it hurt.

No, I responded.

It seemed suddenly like a relief, this budding idea that we could mean something to each other outside of romance. I kept crying quietly, missing my mother, feeling opened for the first time since she died, really. I was looking for a legacy I could hold on to, but no suggestion of a point of origin could replace a real one. Maggie was missing someone, too, I could feel it, maybe a whole world of people.

Maggie slowly pulled her hand out of me, rested her arm on my arm, laid her head on my stomach, listening to it intently, like listening into a shell. We lay like that for a long while, taken care of. Our breathing felt like a body of water, an ocean, swaying continuously, thick and easy.

Could you feel it? I asked eventually.

No, she responded.

Oh no.

No, it's good, remember? That's what you said. You're not supposed to be able to feel it like that, she said.

❀

These days, teenagers don't hang out in the world because they prefer to be on the *internet*. I am still young, not yet thirty, but things have changed in recent years. When I was a child, parents put their children on leashes because we were feral and invested in things like doing a perfect backflip, or finding a good hiding spot under a parked car. The types of risks in which kids are now invested have changed a lot as well. Internet danger is about what happens outside of the body, what the body can't control: private photos that get disseminated nonconsensually while their subject sits helplessly at home; identity theft; a controversial Facebook status update. The children of today ask us post-children: Why go out on a limb and build a fort out of ice that could collapse on you at any moment when you can get the same rush by posting a photo of someone's nipple on Instagram?

Not very long ago, the stakes were in the body. When my mother sent me to my room out of anger, I always tried to put myself in casual distress. For example, I would stand on the dresser and reach up high for something on the top bookshelf that I did not need. This, or I would create a stool out of unstable elements: pillows, a dollhouse, piles of books.

In both cases, I would stand precariously on top and feel very stormy in my heart. The storminess was a tangled combination of shame and self-pity in search of some sort of outcome that would remedy both. Reaching not for the object but for the precariousness of reach itself, I would strain my limbs, becoming long and tall. Two tippy toes, then all my weight on one foot, the big toe, the magical appearance of floating. I would always reach for something, a book or a trinket or a stuffed animal, that I knew was impossibly far away. Then, as always, I would fall tooth-deep into the lip or something as harsh and start to scream. I would lie on the floor and wait for footsteps.

My mother would come cooing, taking me in her arms, and I would bask in the real and fake pain, commingling them into a comforting sense of control and sacrifice. That was when love felt biggest.

Alex said he was heading out early Christmas morning to see his dad for some days but didn't want to hang the night before because he had an early flight. I had chosen to spend Christmas alone in Toronto, but the inevitability of it was becoming daunting. I was confused about whether I wanted to see Maggie; the IUD incident had been the truest moment between us, the moment full of the most tenderness and love. It was Christmas Eve. I messaged her.

Hey do you want to go for a drink or something, I asked, expecting no response.

Ya, I can meet for like an hour, she responded, almost immediately.

I contemplated wearing a sports jacket to our hangout and a pair of embroidered bell bottoms from 100 Percent Silk that were very beautiful. I decided on the pants and a cozy brown knitted sweater, some high-heeled black leather boots, a peacoat, thick-rimmed glasses.

Maggie could pull anything off, her brown leather coats and bright red turtlenecks and her sequined dresses and her beautiful masculine but delicate face and that mouth and the lankiness, something elliptical about her overall, both poised and clunky. It seemed that unless something remarkable happened, I would never be beautiful or ugly in appearance, would never have to stand on either side of that line.

We sat across from each other at a dim bar that smelled of pee and cinnamon, on College and Ossington, blue light and loud Spanish dance music. The energy between us felt new. We held each other by the forearms and stayed that way. She told me that her dad was building her a lion out of putty for Christmas, that she had seen it last week when she was in his apartment.

He's making it look just like the one in this book I liked when I was little, *The Lion, the Witch and the Wardrobe* — it's that lion, she said. I think he fired it and is going to paint in the details. He'll probably give me that and something weird, fur mittens and something, I know he's been working on it for a while. It's really sweet.

Maggie looked at me with her eyes scrunched like she was doing an assessment. The arm holding felt sisterly or friendly, like we were both grateful to be able to talk, grateful for each other. She pulled out her phone.

I'm trying to write a story about him, she said to me. I don't really write stories, but I thought it would be a good Christmas present.

Then Maggie turned the phone toward me and briefly flashed a word document on the screen, as if I could absorb the story like a photograph.

Will you send it to me, I asked.

She smiled in a campy way, all teeth.

I just wrote that his voice was smooth and hollow like a Kinder egg, is that bad writing? she responded. Then she flipped to something else on her phone.

What's the story about?

His birth, she said.

But you weren't there for that.

That's why it's a story.

That's an intense sort of story to write for your father.

Our family doesn't have good boundaries.

That's sweet, I said. My hand started to itch but I didn't move it.

All of my metaphors are about food, though. Anthony Kiedis doesn't use metaphors, she said.

Maggie had stolen *Scar Tissue*, the Anthony Kiedis autobiography, from my shelf a few weeks before. I had read it thrice between the ages of thirteen and sixteen and inundated the margins with notes. I thought then that I would marry him, and so most of the notes in the margins were thoughtful things, conversation points, stuff he might like to talk about. I figured that if I could anticipate all of his desires through the homework of studying his book, the book of his life, then he would overlook my age and lack of fame. This was perhaps the most romantic thing I had ever done for another person, though we never did meet.

He sort of uses a metaphor in the end of his book, on the last line, I said.

Is it a firework?

No, it's about his animal.

I got sad about how quickly he drops all the loves of his life, said Maggie.

Spoiler: he gets a dog.

That's all he deserves, she said.

Ya. I think he was a cool artist at one point because he allowed the psychobabble to flow, I said. Less so later, though.

His pics made me yearn for a brawny fuck.

Ya. Circa 2003.

So snowboard.

Ya.

What I wantchu gotta give it to your dog, she sang.

I think I know how he is in bed, I said.

How?

I can't really explain, but I just know how he would go down on me.

He brags about giving women their first orgasms.

No introspection, I said.

No, Maggie said.

He would, like, arch over you in a way where you know he was picturing himself as if from above.

Maggie let her tongue fall from her mouth and then put it back in.

Search your eyes for the soul both before and after, she said. Dumb.

Dumb is good for precision, I said. You don't want to get too in your head.

Our server, a nondescript guy with tattoos who looked tired, asked us what we wanted to drink. I ordered a pint of Guinness to be cozy and so did Maggie.

Do you think that dumb people are more precise, Maggie asked him in a way that was somehow sexy, innocent, and mean. I watched his eyes flicker, to see if she was flirting. Maggie looked back at me with ardour to tell him that she was not.

Sure, he said, throwing his hands up in the air. Then he walked away.

Anthony seems like someone who would want kids, said Maggie.

You guys are on a first-name basis now, I said.

I like to skip the niceties and get straight to the good stuff, the soulful stuff. The real meat of it, she said, squeezing my wrists.

I thought about Alex, how Maggie's bravery and Alex's easy warmth could make them instantly close. The beer man showed up with our drinks and we broke contact, and I instinctively rubbed my hands together to rid myself of the thought.

You seem like someone who would want kids, I said.

I am someone who would want kids. I think if I got pregnant I would keep it.

The thought of Maggie having a baby made me dizzy.

Is your writing funny, I asked, referring to her short book of erotic poems and also the story she wrote her dad.

I think it's hilarious but whenever I read it aloud, no one laughs. Last time I did a reading, I read the funniest one, which was about the different sorts of sounds lovers make together. One woman broke down crying in the middle of my reading and said it was the most heartbreaking thing she had ever heard. Beep beep, choo choo.

You want to be sad funny.

I don't *want* sad funny, she said, looking away, as if punishing me for failing to understand something fundamental.

Why?

I can't control it if I try and be light and it makes someone upset. That's the opposite of what I want. Everyone is so different from everyone else.

We went for a cigarette. Haloed by orange light, Maggie's frame seemed to melt the snow around her. We made quiet eye contact for a long time and moved through different phases of recognition. Our eyes made questions at each other, and then they made answers. We took risks with our eye contact, and then it got sexy, and then it got stupid, and then we both started laughing and couldn't stop. I closed my eyes and when I reopened them, her loveliness was still somehow a shock, her easy laughter. The second I accepted her beauty outside of some union between us it felt almost too lovely to bear, sending me back to the part that wanted to hold on tight. When we got back in the bar I expected us to get another round, but she had to go, got up and paid for both of us, suddenly a bit impersonal, rushed.

Where are you going, I asked, sort of drunk. Do you want to come over?

I can't, she responded, kissing both my cheeks. Love you, I hope your Christmas is okay.

Thanks, okay, love you, too, I said. We hadn't said that before.

I watched her leave and time and distance collided, and suddenly it seemed difficult, the walk from the bar to the subway stop, the subway to home. My ideal night, I realized, wouldn't be sleeping with Maggie, but something else: maybe we play a safety game where we pretend that the ground is lava and so we need to keep reaching for the spaces above the drop, taking great care all the while. I thought of us as babies again, like she said, so close in age, moving through the world in different people's arms all the time, limbs outstretched like we knew how to fly.

The first Christmas after Alex's mom left, he and Robert Delaney came to church with me and my mom and dad. Mom surveyed the group about whether we should go to church or to the *Lord of the Rings* movie, and for some reason I chose church. So did Robert and my mom, while my dad and Alex chose *Lord of the Rings*. In the end, church won, but my dad fell asleep moments into the service and snored so loudly that we had to escort him out of there early. Sorry God, I hiss-whispered on my way out, and my mom bopped me with her hip.

We all went back to my house for food and drinks afterward. Mom made charcuterie and let us take B52 shots even though we were only twelve. Naturally, Robert Delaney loved B52 shots, the calm way in which the milky liquor cascaded down and the way that the colours separated into three distinct warm retro shades in the shot glass. Mom knew how to use a spoon to pour them properly. My dad commented on how his wasn't really separating, and she told him, You'll have to fire me. Then, when Robert cheersed to his missing wife, Alex's mother, whose name was Rosalie, my mom looked at him with a smile that betrayed a deep sympathy and told him he was cunt-struck. It was risky and also the first time I saw him laugh since Rosalie left.

It's still hard to explain my mother and how she was, and every time I try to I get stuck, because it's impossible to sum up that sort of love. I knew then that she was special because she knew herself so deeply, and in knowing herself she knew just how to love everyone in the most meaningful way, it seemed. She knew how to give people space and how to fill it in even when they didn't think they wanted it filled. And she never seemed to feel like anyone was watching her, never seemed worried about what that could mean, even though she was poised and sophisticated in a big way, too. I remember going to the library, how if there was a book she wanted on the bottom shelf, she would lie down on the floor to get it, and if a stranger walked past, she would tell them, simply, to walk over her. She knew how to be funny or supportive in the right way when someone was hurting; if a friend had a spouse or child die, we would pick up KFC and a bottle of whiskey and drop them on the front step, because she said fried chicken was good grief food, the perfect thing to eat when you didn't want to think about cooking or really think about food at all. She said it would keep the meat on your bones.

That night, as we all sat in the deep orange light of the family room and listened to Patsy Cline, the absence of Rosalie was thick in the air. The thing was, my mom knew things that other people didn't know, somehow. She knew, for example, that Robert was a wonderful singer and that singing was the most cathartic thing to him. He didn't sing often, but she had this information stored inside of her. Alex sat next to me and we drank our B52s, which tasted better than I thought they would, and a little like medicine. After talking for a while, my mom ushered me over to the corner by the bar.

I'm going to put on a song, she said, and we're all going to leave the room except for Alex's dad, okay? Just for the song.

Why, I asked.

You'll see, she responded. Tell Alex.

I sat back down next to Alex and whispered it to him. We got up and went to the hall. Then a moment later, my mom pulled my dad into the hall, too. Robert sat there alone, a few drinks in, and then something amazing happened. My mother, ever so slightly, started turning up the speaker, and the song "Crazy" by Patsy Cline got louder and louder in the room. And as the words grew from murmurs to bellows in our ears, I started to hear something else I hadn't noticed in the song before:

a deep harmony, low and warbling. I looked in and there was Robert, harmonizing Patsy beautifully and with everything he had, eyes wet and slow breaths coming from the depths of his stomach. He sang the verses about being crazy for loving her, his voice aching like Leonard Cohen, like he might start bawling at any moment. He filled the room, filled up all of the space in it, lit it up like bioluminescence at the drop of an oar, the energy cascading outward and into the hallway, out to all of us secret onlookers.

Slowly, we all walked back into the room as the song was ending, and Mom went to Robert, put her small hand on his giant shoulder, and with his other arm he hooked Alex in, despite Alex's squirming, and hugged him into his side. I leaned into my mother's shoulder and my dad sat to my right. I knew the moment couldn't last, but that it would last forever in a way, too.

I don't think I really believe in God, said Alex then. Which is why I was hoping to see the movie. So I'm happy we didn't have to stay at church, but this is pretty good, too, he said, rubbing the cold skin on his arm.

My mom wrapped a blanket around him.

That's all right my darlin', she said. But for the love of God eat something — you're getting so lanky that soon you won't be fit to shoot.

It felt sad to go home on Christmas Eve when my apartment didn't feel like a destination, didn't really feel like somewhere to be. What reward was waiting there? There was no reward waiting there, just a normal bed that had nothing of the holiday spirit in it, normal groceries for breakfast, Lionel. Outside the street lights zigzagged and became nondescript, trapped in my eyelashes. A light snow had fallen but there was barely anyone outside, few footprints, giving the city a strange, fake feeling, like a village inside of a snow globe.

I thought of how Newfoundland would probably be the first province underwater what with the sad projected future of the world. Would I be alive to watch it sink from my laptop? I had a bottle of wine in my backpack, which I realized I had subconsciously packed on the off chance that Maggie would invite me over once and for all, that she would let me see her room now that things were different between us.

Rather than going home, I started walking to a vantage point I liked — it was the roof of a restaurant called People's Eatery, on Spadina, that you could climb up to easily from behind the building. The remarkable thing about the roof wasn't just its easy access, but the fact that on top one room had a skylight, and if you looked down, some apartment or office or generally nondescript space had this room full of giant fish tanks; if you went at night, no one was ever down below, but the fish tanks emanated a blue-green glow up through the skylight, and since the skylights were pitched on a relatively steep angle, you could lean against them, huddled, basking in this otherworldly light (which was also next to an air vent that let out warm air, making the spot warm in the winter). Alex and I spent a lot of time up there in the summer as well drinking bottles of wine, dangling our feet, watching people walk below us, smoking, trying not to flick ash on their heads.

I closed my eyes a few times and pressed my fingers against my eyelids, exploding the private abstract patterns in colourful fireworks, the pressure of my fingers creating them. People say it's bad to do this, but no one was around to tell me not to, and I was an adult. Apparently DMT releases a drug in your brain that you otherwise experience only when you die, and it is that drug that creates all of the crazy, symmetrical, multicoloured universes that you see when you google things like "acid trip," the most clichéd of images; and they are shared among the public with the release of this chemical, this death feeling. I wondered if my mother had experienced that, had lived a life drug-free only to have chaotic rave imagery bombard her in the last moment, some final joke, or maybe some final tidy slice of beauty, made only joke-like by its relation to psychedelic drugs.

When I got to the back of the closed restaurant, I remembered there was one part of the climb that I had forgotten and that was sort of difficult to do. Once you climb up the side awning of the first building, you have to jump between two flat surfaces that are on the same plane but a few feet apart, in between them, a long and narrow drop into a garbagey alleyway, probably full of rats and needles. A dirty, angry slice of forgotten land.

I looked up and the moon was a sliver, a little hook on its edge covered by a cloud, as if the cloud were hanging there, appeasing the moon by making it think that it couldn't hang out like that all by itself, that it needed the moon's hooked edge to hold it upright. I laughed and started to whistle. *The moon is so smug*, I thought. I thought about the jump and a private question fluttered in me — *Was it worth putting yourself in a precarious situation if no one could see you do it, or find you moments later and tell you it was okay?*

I made the jump anyways, felt my heart become my throat, my ears, temples, my whole body becoming a heart for a minute there. Jumping into the future, imagining the future as a past, underwater. The snow was falling so gently, the city so quiet, the smell of garbage in the distance. But barely — cold doesn't carry much with it. After the jump there is one more gentle incline up the side of a roof, and then you turn at the top of it, shimmy down, and voila: you're on a flat surface, next to the sky window, awash in all of that blue flooding light.

I heard the sound of shimmying, a big animal maybe, probably just a raccoon but maybe something bigger than a raccoon. Could it hurt me? Would it want to? I edged my way over the top of the roof and looked down to the blue light, ready for anything.

Except I wasn't. And there it was: Maggie and Alex, kissing in a big way, hands under jackets. Alex was back on, his shiny hair glinting in the stark light, Maggie facing toward me, her long delicate fingers snaking up the back of his neck. I let out some noise, wanting to do anything to make it stop, to bring myself to voice outside of language, glossolalic. Together they were a strange animal and it was hurting me. When I closed my eyes, a kaleidoscope of Maggie and Alex kissing presented itself, perfectly symmetrical and spinning, my mind eager to make the image a tidy fiction, sacred geometry like the death drug, ending a story, closing it up. I couldn't believe it and I could. Of course. Like in the movie *The Breakfast Club,* where they all start and end the same way: a jock, a princess, a delinquent, et cetera, despite what had unfolded through that day, everything and nothing having changed, the characters simply restored to their own fates despite development or budding interdependency. Betrayal as realizing something is right where you left it. I started to cry, to sob, the tears quickly freezing onto my cheeks, forgetting for a moment that they would unfreeze, that time would continue persisting or unfolding, however you want to believe in it, how it moves.

Alex heard the sound of me.

Sophie, he said, spinning back.

But by then I was inching back down the side of the awning, moving toward the space between the two buildings.

Go fuck yourselves, I said, looking back at both of them, and then I leapt forward from one awning to the other, clearing the gap and landing painfully, absorbing the shock in my ankles and knees and up and up, knees shaking as if to shake it out like grief shaken out, like a game like a die like dice like monopoly pieces, sharp and other, the bucking horse, a thimble.

I took a shortcut through a side alley so that they wouldn't find me and remembered how Alex had saved me that night in junior high, the air offensively cold and still as this night, and how so many Christmas Eves had that same stillness, with my mom quietly wrapping gifts last-minute in the room adjacent while I tried to keep my eyes closed, and how my desire for Maggie had felt exciting and still and out of time like those nights waiting to fall asleep before I got caught wide-eyed with my empty stocking at the head of the bed, but even those times in childhood had a destination, the destination being a space of sleep and then waking to some bright tradition, and now that was all gone, and there was nothing to make a noise at, and there was nothing to move toward except the night, no thick or sustaining ardour, no open arms, no best friend, no fear because I was in it, no fear except the fear of inside, no fear except the fear of the space that housed it, no fear in finding out, because the thing about fear is that part of me already knew, part of me had already felt at home in the feeling before I even arrived, and that was the worst part.

Part Two

THE ART CASTLE WAS AN UNRESTORED CONVENT IN Saint-Erme, in the Champagne region of France, where people, mainly performance artists but also writers and musicians and visual artists and dancers, lived for times spanning from two days to their whole lives. Its shape was a Tetris *C*, or maybe more like a sideways Tetris *U*, with a courtyard outside between the connected buildings, full of picnic tables. I opened the window of the piano room and sat on its ledge. Light snow fell onto my knees, a peacock walked past. Did the peacock understand English, or French, or neither? Did it understand its own beauty?

On a whim, I had followed Lionel, who came here to work on his novel, even though I was feeling very post-Lionel. I was over enjoying the company of Lionel, but I knew how to be near him without feeling pain, which seemed good enough for now.

I had been commissioned for a massive glass project for a restaurant owned by a man named Dave Garcia, whom people

called the million-dollar taco man because he owned so many
Mexican restaurants in Toronto. The glass project was a two-
hundred-square-foot series of doors, several agave plants rendered in glass and climbing a wall of a restaurant at Yonge
and Eglington, a rich area of Toronto where even the air outside ominously smelled like airport. It was not a flat-surface
project but, rather, one where the mosaics were to frame all
of the doors, going up the walls next to the doors, and along
the ceiling as well. I was able to get the glass materials sent
for not much money considering the cost of commission, and
ultimately I decided it would be good to finish all I could in
France over the course of a month, bring the mosaics back,
and complete them on-site. It was mid-January, and I had until
April to mount and grout the mosaics. At first the cost and details of travel seemed frivolous and cumbersome, but they were
paying fifteen thousand dollars for the project in full, and the
return flight from Paris was only six hundred dollars, with an
extra fee of four hundred dollars for sending the materials. One
thousand dollars to not feel insane and lonely in Toronto while
Maggie and Alex burrowed into their heaven-scape of romance
seemed a fair cost.

Lots of people at the castle had read Ben Lerner; Ben Lerner
came up a few times. I had just read *The Topeka School* and
10:04, and I was thinking a lot about Ben. I read *The Topeka
School* first, and then *10:04*. I wanted to read the other one but
I felt like *The Topeka School* blew my mind entirely, while *10:04*
was less good and actually very annoying at points. I talked to
maybe six people about Ben Lerner, and they all had differ-
ing opinions about which book they liked best. A German sex
worker/dance choreographer, Norbert, liked *Leaving the Atocha
Station* best, while Nico, a performance artist, liked *10:04*.

What I realized after a bit was that actually, each person loved the book that they read first without realizing it. I asked them which one they loved most, they talked about it, and then later I asked them what order they read the books in. It was always the first one that they found mind-blowing, and then the others sort of lacklustre.

Lionel and I talked about this and agreed on the fact that something about reading a bunch of Ben Lerner in a row pulled some sort of curtain down on his magic. It was like, at a certain point, you understand how he's doing what he's doing. The smoke and mirrors are gone, and suddenly his writing starts to feel too clever, too self-referential, as if the formula is some algorithm of repeated images that turn back in on themselves, like he (the author) is winking, but not at you and only sort of at himself. Winking into the void. Lionel said that he really didn't like in *10:04* when Ben (or the speaker) discussed his own poetry. There is a whole section of the book where the speaker in Ben's book, also named Ben, is working at a writing residency and writes one very long poem about his time there. He transcribes much of that poem into the book itself.

I think it's cocky, said Lionel. The idea that you can put your own work into your work, call it work within work. It's embarrassing, like framing your own drawing over the fireplace. It's a kid's thing, he said, sitting on a tall chair in the large kitchen, kicking at the rusting metal legs.

The art castle was a strange place to be, as if out of time. Because of its seclusion, no one really left the property on day trips, making the whole thing sort of microcosmic, like being on reality TV. Everyone at the castle was pretty psycho and good-looking, I thought. One woman just did performance art with couches: she collected all the couches into one room and asked the participants to let the couch act upon them. I participated in this early one morning and ended up lying flat on my back on the cold morning concrete, supporting the weight of an entire couch with my torso. Things like that. A lot of philosophers awoke with the sun to try and summon the spirit of Hegel.

A man named Brutus would often come by to look at the glass project I was working on and say things like, It's nice that some art doesn't have to be interesting, doesn't even have to be art really, just has to be pretty. And then he would leave.

Once I showed Brutus a completed tile, and he said he liked it because it filled his mind with a vast nothingness.

The vibe of the castle was punctuated by the fact that its owner, a seventy-year-old man named Benoit who had run the convent (we called it an art castle but really it was an old convent) for forty years, had been "me too'd" the previous year and then promptly diagnosed with terminal lung cancer, as if all of his bad habits were culminating here at the end to teach him a lesson. It was early winter, but he was scheduled to die by the fall. As a self-run progressive "school" of sorts, the people attending the art castle constantly set up shows for whatever their project was (from philosophy presentations about Derrida to performance art to dance to DJ sets), and the events ran every night, sometimes overlapping, approximately one hundred residents in the castle at all times.

Whereas I had heard that at one point Benoit roamed the halls with optimistic vigour, excited to see the creations of the artists he housed and never bored of their cumulatively mundane absurdity, by now he was mainly invested in wreaking havoc among the living. He had been fine living out his legacy in glory, but when people started to call him a bad man, he soured, unable to understand the nuance of those claims or unwilling to face them, the collection of his life's greatness boiled down to being a creepy old letch with bad politics. When someone showed a short film that they made years earlier, Benoit walked in halfway through, guffawing and flailing his hands, afterward asking some unproductive question about why the filmmaker didn't, say, use a different narrative technique in the making of the film, why she didn't angle the camera downward from the top corner of the room to articulate the fishbowl-esque quality of the protagonist's paranoia, for example, the sorts of criticism that, of course, everyone knew couldn't be fixed in a movie that had already been released in 2010 and was being shown more for entertainment than critique.

I thought of Benoit's predicament as somehow parallel to the poetry in Ben Lerner's novels. Maybe I thought of this parallel because Ben and Benoit sort of both had the same name, but as I watched Benoit, some seventy years old, tall and lanky, with long grey hair, clearly a charmer and a hottie in his time, when I watched him slowly walk through the yard alone, feeding his fuzzy baby chicks, pondering to himself, a sour look on his face, I thought about him getting trapped in this exposing limbo, the space between an old mythologized identity and a sobering new one.

There's that Anne Carson line, "To live past your myth is a perilous thing," but what about getting stuck between it, where the qualities that made you a certain kind of person were taken up later and re-explained, transforming you into something else culturally, something outside of your own control? It is this sort of sociopolitical shift that is responsible for the most important collective work ever, giving voice to the disenfranchised. It's the good work. Still, it's weird to watch on the individual level, to see someone as a result of it slip between the cracks of their own life. Benoit's characteristics didn't change necessarily, until the repetition of them through a shifting societal context brought him down, which ultimately changed him. All of the potential poetry of his existence lost its charge, embarrassing him. He was a symbol trapped between two contexts.

At different points, people seem to get sick of themselves, how they are in real life. I wondered about this with Alex and Maggie, secretly hoped that maybe the intrigue that had brought them together would make them romanticize each other too much, so that when they actually settled into a relationship, the reality wouldn't measure up to the ideas they had of each other. My mental health wasn't great.

Other than work, my goal at the art castle was to become more worldly by flirting with a lot of people. I had my own room at the art castle, replete with a little sleigh bed, a big opening window, a sink, a mirror, a closet, and a desk. The wallpaper on the walls was a faded pink with tiny rosebuds, but in some spots the wallpaper peeled open like petals, revealing two other layers of wallpaper, one blue and striped, the other a light yellow with different flowers. The layers of wallpaper, all of them equally pretty and dirty and delicate, gave me a hopeful feeling. On the first day in my room, I closed the door, washed the floor with Dr. Bronner's lavender soap and paper towel and water, sat on the windowsill and smoked a cigarette and waited for the floor to dry, and then I lay down on it.

Once I had lain in one spot on the floor, I moved over to the next vacant spot, trying to cover the whole floor at one point or another with my body, legs closed, arms above my head. If there was room, I would just roll 180 degrees onto my next spot on the floor. I did this without any clothing on. The floor was

still damp and a little sticky. Depressed, I peeled my body off
the floor like a sticker and then moved to a new spot, lay down
there, and stared at the ceiling for so long that I felt dizzied by
the idea that it wasn't a wall.

Eventually I got up, dried off with a towel, and took naked
photos with my phone timer, sending them to no one. In the
photos, I am sprawled prostrate on the tiny bed, my arms dangling over the side. I look too young, and a little bit asleep.

The photos are sort of sexy, still. In the background of
them, an anachronistic-seeming box of Corn Flakes, the room
being unrestored and one hundred years old, me being naked
and thus timeless. I liked the idea of becoming a new woman
with a different sort of soul, and so the idea of doing something
special for the purpose of telling no one.

Maggie had written me a bunch, Alex just once. Alex said
this:

> Dear Sophie,
> Hi. I'm really sorry that you had to find out
> about me and Maggie that way. I was feeling
> weird and confused about it for a while and
> didn't know what to say to you, and I didn't
> want to say anything if it was nothing, or if
> it turned out to be nothing. It always seems
> like giving bad news occurs either too early or
> too late, like there's no good time for it. I love
> you so much and I don't want to risk our bond
> for the sake of another person, even though I
> realize it might be too late for that. You're the
> most important person to me in all of life, and
> if there's a chance that you'll forgive me, if that

means that you don't want her and me to see each other then I will stop doing that. I feel strongly about her and I know you don't want to hear about that but I do. I don't know, it's weird, there's something going on that I don't really know how to articulate. It doesn't feel small. But I can squish it, if that's what you want and need. I don't know what to say really, I realize that this puts you in a weird and painful spot, which I didn't want, and would never want. I feel really mixed up. I told Maggie that I couldn't see her until I heard back from you, but even telling you that makes me feel like I'm trying to sound good when I know that anything good I could say or do at this point is predicated on me doing a bad thing, or maybe not bad, but hurtful. I love you. Take your time, please let me know if you want to talk, I'll be standing by.

Xo, love

Alex

Alex had sent this email on New Year's after sending a shorter text version of it on Boxing Day and leaving several voice mails to call him, and so it had been almost a month and I hadn't responded. What was I supposed to say? I told Lionel about it, and he had no advice that acknowledged the beauty of either Alex or Maggie. I told him this, and he said that when people hurt you, it's in your best interest to avoid acknowledging such complexity, that it's better to blunt the nuances of the heart when you're hurt and trying to protect yourself, because everyone is teeming with contradiction, and it's crazy-making to hold all of a person at once when you're trying to figure out what to do about the pain that they've caused you. I told Lionel that this wouldn't work, that I wasn't in the business of wilful forgetfulness.

Well then, maybe you have to tell them not to be together, said Lionel while cutting a potato into thin strips on a wooden cutting board in the giant communal kitchen.

Whenever Lionel cooked, there appeared to be some sort of potential toward a finished product — chopped vegetables, a pot boiling. But then usually when he was done making whatever he was working on, it just resulted in the worst version of food. He would probably put these finely julienned potato strips into a bowl of hot water with hot sauce in it and call it soup, for example.

I thought about emailing Alex to tell him to stop seeing Maggie, but then I thought, *What would that even do?* Then I would be that friend who kept people from their truest desires for my own sake. Keeping them apart would in no way make each of them less aware of the other's beauty, of which they were already aware. If anything, it would allow them both to preserve their beauty, trapping romance at its clearest point of potential, the spot where it wants to be most.

Maggie sent me different sorts of messages over the weeks, none of them containing apologies. For example, first Maggie sent a picture of herself in her new tank top. The tank top said "Miami" in pink eighties font.

I am a gay man, she wrote to me. Then she wrote, Help.

The next week, Maggie wrote:

> I cried at the pool today. I got to the pool
> and realized I had forgotten my bathing suit.
> Like what the fuck. I know you would have

reminded me. The weather keeps changing and I feel like a cat. It's warm-hot out, for winter. I feel like I'm losing it. You can feel how the world is ending. I looked in through the glass at the YMCA, at all of the swimmers in their perfect order, and started to cry, so I left. Like they were on the other side of something and I couldn't get to it. I miss you, you're grounding. You're really special.

A week later, Maggie wrote:

My roommate Cory threw my painting out the window today. The one I've been working on for six years. And he stole four hundred dollars from Cotey. Cory and Jonah are breaking up. I think for real this time. Cory yelled at me in the kitchen, like really screamed a lot. I think Jonah's gonna move back to Montreal. Cotey is fucked and he's letting young hot men come into our house to buy coke instead of meeting them by the library. He's trying to seduce them with the drugs so there's people everywhere. I left lasagna on the counter and these two little baby Leo DiCaprio boys were there just eating it the next minute, vaping DMT. I don't feel great about this as a home environment.

The painting Maggie had been working on for years was fifty square feet and had tiny images of the faces of every person she ever met on it. It was really remarkable, except I had never seen it in person because she never let me come to her house, because she said she didn't have a bed frame and if I ever went inside I'd never want to see her again.

Most recently, Maggie wrote: I love you. I have a little bird ornament and I called it Sophie. I tell it stories. It's quiet but it listens.

Although I didn't answer any of Maggie's messages at first, she treated it as if I was responding to her, like we were having some sort of normal correspondence. Every time I read a note from her, I lay on the floor of my bedroom, staring at the ceiling until my heart shrank back down to a heart size and stopped consuming my body. Her messages made me think about sanctimony. Alex's email had made me want to be good, to tell them that they had my blessing, that I wanted them to be happy. But I held off, worrying that, in fact, this was just a power move on my part and that there was no real merit in my approval if I secretly wanted them to fail, which a big part of me did. But Maggie's messages did something else: they talked me down from my little theoretical tower, talked me down from my anger while simultaneously making me feel frustrated (how dare she be so chill?), created a self-reflexive dialogue, no power of giving or receiving an apology.

In many moments, the whole thing was exhausting, trying to wrangle my feelings into some sort of conclusion. How is a person supposed to feel when the two most beautiful people in their life do something that results in them acting in a hurtful way? Could they mainly coexist outside of the phantom limb of my disapproval? Why was it so easy to feel like a potential liability the second you risk being outnumbered? Was I even that important to them at all? And why ask me if, as Alex said, the whole thing would not continue without my sanction? Maybe he was lying.

But in some special moments I felt hopeful and resolved to the idea that both Maggie and Alex were considering me as some sort of central force in their union, like an unborn child. In one such moment, I curled into the fetal position on my bed and stared out the window, watching the sun bleed open the sky and slowly lower itself to sleep. In moments like that one, I felt lucky and less alone in the world, weirdly less alone than I even did before I found out about them.

One night I had sex with Norbert, the German choreographer, and his long shiny chestnut hair and his manicured nails and his shirt with all of the rave graphics on it. Norbert looked like a porn star, eighties moustache. There was boxed wine and communal dinner at the big indoor picnic table and off-tune piano karaoke and sweaty dancing in a high-ceilinged parlour hall, and there was slick closeness and bodies swaying together like algae on the ocean floor, and there was Norbert leaning into my back. He told me he was a man but also that he felt like a lesbian. I couldn't figure out whether he was being really progressive or the opposite, but it didn't really matter at that juncture, the juncture where I was drunk and wanted to have sex, and he came back to my room and kissed me, tangling my hair up loosely in his big hand.

Doggy style seemed more North American, while it seemed more European to ravage someone, to really take their whole face into your face, like my face was falling and his was catching it. I closed my eyes and pictured us as if from above, looking down, like I thought Anthony Kiedis might do. I saw my naked back, my small hands pressed against Norbert's shoulders. *There are people who I love, and they're in a different country, and they're thinking about me, too*, I thought. I let Norbert take my hair into a tight ponytail, got on my knees, took him in my mouth, drool pooling down my chin.

Afterward, Norbert said, Thank you.

I hated to be thanked for sex but let it slide. Then he told me about his complicated relationship to his grandmother, who had been a Nazi.

Do you say that to all the girls, I asked Norbert, and he said no, but I knew that he probably did post-coitally tell all the girls about his nana. I kissed Norbert's big nose and then gracefully ushered him out of the room, closed the door quietly, got into bed.

In the night a bat flew in through my window and started circling the ceiling of my bedroom. I tried pointing at it and saying, Hey that's not cool, you have to go now! The circles made me dizzy. The bat couldn't see, but it could intuit the corners of the room and never smashed into anything.

In the morning, my room was cold, a sharp breeze running through it. I got up to close the window and noticed outside that there were little red flowers in the snow, roses or carnations, peeking up through the white. The image reminded me of global warming, not as a concept but, rather, as its ubiquitous stake on everything. Soon, any sort of environmental paradox would be taken as expected sensory information. I tried to give these moments, moments where I was reacquainted with the world's imminent end, a brief few seconds of silence, to feel the weight of it in my arms and legs. I wanted, in that moment, to be like the main character in the Chantal Akerman film *Je Tu Il Elle*, the girl who sits alone in a room for months and does nothing but write letters and eat bags of sugar with her spoon, undone by her grief.

Loving comes with its fair share of fear, but sometimes people possess such beauty that in loving them the stakes of loss are so high that the fear overtakes the joy to a staggering degree. I think that this soulful beauty comes down to saying yes to life at every corner. My mother was like this. She had experienced such loss in her life, had lost her own mother and her brother at such young and unexpected ages, yet she was teeming with life. One of the last questions I asked her was what her favourite age was. She was standing, facing me, eating Froyo and wearing a fluorescent orange coat that she had gotten on sale for twenty dollars but was too big for her.

That's a lot of coat and not a lot of me, she said. Then she looked at me and said, Well, your age is good. Twenty-five. I loved being twenty-five. And I loved being forty. And even now, sixty-five. Every age is amazing.

Lionel and I met for lunch in the dining room and made cheese sandwiches and coffee. While most people at the castle were beautiful and svelte, it didn't seem like anyone ate many fruits or vegetables. I had been feeling hopeful but also mostly depressed, long days in the studio cutting tiny squares of glass one after another and gluing them to the wedi board, a waterproof material that has cement on either side and Styrofoam in between and is lightweight enough to make glass mosaics relatively easy to transport. My fingers were chafed and cut up, and my back ached excessively in the night, like I was one hundred years old. I had given up on the beauty of food and was trying, mainly, to survive.

Lionel looked at me for a moment with an alarming pause. His general nature was not to fear saying something that upset another person. Once he outright asked me if I had taken a hammer to his bicycle without considering the fact that such a question might be hurtful. So his look of concern threw me.

What is it, Lionel, I asked. Benoit skulked past us and headed for the stairs, likely going up to the lecture hall to see the early afternoon interpretive dance recital.

I love food, said Lionel. Onion, tomatoes, celery.

Okay.

I think it is something I feel passionately about.

Cooking?

No, but describing food. Chocolate chips, raspberries, tuna.

Gross. Okay, cool.

Lionel took a breath and held his cheese sandwich in front of him in a prestigious way.

I think, you see, I think, instead of finishing my novel, I'm going to stay in France and, um, become a food critic. I think it is what I, um, must do, instead of returning to Toronto. I've thought about it. You can sublet my room out. I will come back in the summer and deal with my things, but I will not be returning to Toronto ... in the meantime, he said.

Lionel, you don't know anything about food, I said, suddenly nauseous. You never go to restaurants, and you only cook three different types of meals, all of which are very basic. Plus you're colour-blind. Do you really think that forgoing your rent-stabilized apartment in the city where you live is a good idea right now? Have you thought about this? What am I supposed to do, also? We're supposed to return in a week.

I've thought about this, said Lionel. I've thought it through and it's what I must do.

I looked at Lionel to see if he was kidding. He blinked at me and nodded his head, as if the matter was settled. I knew that the second I left France, he would not be sending me any more rent, regardless of whether I found someone to take his room in seven days or not.

I threw the other half of my sandwich in the garbage and started to march off. Lionel stood there seemingly unfazed by our interaction, continuing to eat his cheese sandwich. His calmness made me even angrier.

Coward! I yelled, and slammed the door, which swung back on its hinges and knocked over a fern.

After smoking three cigarettes outside next to the peacocks and punishing myself in the cold winter air without putting on a sweater, I went to see the interpretive dance. My hands were vibrating, but there was little to be done, locked into the general quietude of the castle with no way to expend my rage.

The dance was between a very young and frail-looking woman named Gertrude and an older bald man whose name I did not know. Everyone sat in a circle on the floor around the room, and Gertrude and the man silently navigated their way around each other's bodies. The man placed several tangerines on supine Gertrude's torso and thighs and then covered her in a net. Then he arched over her, pulsing like a heart, as she slowly moved her chest up higher and higher, closer to him, somehow continuing to balance the tangerines on her body as she moved. This went on for some time, until the man covered

Gertrude in a dark grey sheet and disturbingly appeared to rape the body under the sheet. At this point you could no longer see Gertrude and could only see the spastic movements she was making under the sheet, in apparent attempt to escape the man. When the man "came," he slowed down his rhythmic movements on top of her and slowly pulled the curtain away from her body. The end of the performance revealed Gertrude lying on her back, all five of the tangerines now in a bunch on her stomach, as if she was pregnant with a tangerine baby. When it was over, everyone clapped.

After the clapping, there was a question and answer period, where Gertrude and the man asked how the performance could be improved and what people's general take-away was. Some people said it seemed to be a thrashing tale of lust, desire, and trauma that ended with new life and hope, which I found to be a fucked-up interpretation. Many men commented on the exciting nature of Gertrude and the man's chemistry, that they were in love. Lionel said something to this effect.

I felt my face get hot and tight. Then I heard a familiar voice. It was saying:

Are you fucking kidding me? They're not in LOVE. He RAPED her, you fucking morons! If she's pregnant it's not with a LOVE baby, it's with a RAPE baby; it's not a NICE ENDING to the story, you LOSERS!

It was my own voice.

All went silent except for the sound of a dusty guffaw in the corner. Benoit sat there, the only person on a chair, shaking his head and staring at me with hatred. He looked, I realized, sort of like the peacocks, his long neck and delicate frame and large pointed nose. He sat wearing an aquamarine silk robe, his blue eyes shining violently.

•

What is it with you young Americans and things, always saying any art is just political, always taking the barest and most animal message from a thing of beauty, he opined in his thick French accent. Why cannot you let for the nuance of creation; why is everyone saying, oh rape this, rape that? It sickens me. There is more to art than just this idea that it is morally question.

The room seemed to close in on itself. I looked around for support but everyone cast their eyes downward.

So we're just supposed to overlook a thing like rape in performance and call it love? I asked.

Benoit looked past me, out the window, affecting some false wisdom.

Silly girl, he said. You know nothing of art or suffering.

I'm sorry that my generation's "political awareness" doesn't take rape lightly, okay? I'm sorry that you rapists are no longer able to get away with the fun you used to have before people cared about stuff like that. It must be awfully *inconvenient* for you, must feel pretty *invasive*! If you're going to feel personally attacked by it, I mean, which you obviously do, which just proves my point.

By the time my voice shut off and I realized, as if watching from above, that I had stopped speaking, I felt the cheese sandwich thick in my throat. Some people were awkwardly getting up and leaving the room one by one. I felt really sick.

Benoit looked at me with a tired expression full of sorrow. Then he pursed his lips shut, and I saw tears collect in his eyes. I hated him. He got up and left the room. I threw up in a wastebasket near the door. Everyone was gone. I was disgusted at them, the fact that no one had anything to add, no one had the courage to back me up. These were not my friends; these were the people of the castle, people who did a lot of ketamine

and spent entire years of their lives doing things like painting shadows of chairs and tables on the walls behind them in
sheep's blood.

I eventually got up and walked like a ghost to my room.
Technically it was Benoit's room, a room owned by Benoit,
Benoit the slutty old philanderer whom I had just called a rapist. I sat in the middle of my bed for a long time, unable to
move. Eventually I heard a knock. It was Norbert and his big
wide open face. Norbert sat down on the bed next to me.

Listen, I appreciate what you were trying to do in there.
And everyone gets it, said Norbert. But you have to understand, he's alone, and he's dying. He's on his way out, okay?
Reminding him of his failures at this juncture, I get why you
would want to do it, and I don't want to tell you what to do,
but maybe that is energy better saved for someone who is going
to live.

I smooshed my left foot under my right foot and felt like
a child.

How do you know who is going to live, Norbert, I asked,
pulling my body away from the contact of his hand.

I guess you don't know who is going to live, but in this case,
you know who isn't going to live. I mean, except for while he's
alive, which is now.

I don't feel sorry for what I said, and it's not really your
business, just because we fucked.

I understand how you're feeling, Sophie, really.

There's no way that you do, I responded.

Okay, well, either way. Maybe just leave the old guy alone,
hey? In the future. There's no changing his mind about anything now. Trying to is just misery for all parties.

You can go now, I said.

After Norbert left, I sat in my room for many hours. I looked back at the email from Alex and the ones from Maggie. I didn't want to die alone in my tall castle, full of sanctimony.

Maggie had sent one more message:

> Sophie. I picture you in a literal castle with a moat and a big flag. When you come back, I can't help but think that you'll have this really long hair, longer than your height. I want to brush it, and sometimes I think about dyeing it different colours. I'm really sad today, because my chaos house is disbanding. Cory and Jonah are breaking up, and Cory stole five hundred dollars from Zinc, and he's losing it. It isn't good here. My gay frat boys are no longer a stable family. You feel more like family than any of it right now. I hope you feel big and bright and happy. Sending love.

I read the message over and over again. Then I wrote Alex:

> Hi Alex.
> Sorry I've been quiet for so long, I've been needing to protect my heart. I think you and Maggie should be together, if that's what you want. I'll be back in a week. It will be weird to see you guys and I don't know if it will feel easy but I'm up for trying. I miss you. I don't trust you in a logistical way rn but I trust you in a fundamental way that has to do with your soul. I'll talk to you soon.

I spent the next couple of days avoiding Lionel and quietly moving between my bedroom and the studio where I was doing the glass mosaic. While I didn't complete the whole project, it was about 80 percent done, which was likely more than I would have completed in Canada. Residencies were good for working, but not necessarily in a peaceful oasis way like I had thought, and more in a prison sort of way where you're like, *Well what else am I going to do in here?*

On my third to last night in the art castle, from my bedroom window I saw Benoit walking through the garden. He pressed his fingers against the mysterious flowers planted in the snowy hill, and I wondered whether it was painful to see something thrive despite its context, as a person on the brink of having no context at all. I walked down to the garden and found him farther away, near the chicken coop, feeding the tiny baby chicks. He was pulling little pieces of food from his coat pocket and inserting them directly into the mouths of the fuzzy chicks, the softest little creatures in the whole world who had no idea about either of us or our flaws.

I'm sorry I called you a rapist, I said. I don't think ...

He put his hand up to stop me and smiled a tiny bit. Then he resumed feeding the chicks, cooing at them gently. I felt in that moment that we had both become symbols to each other and that time was running out. He was looking for some final instances of beauty and would find none between us.

On my way back to my room, I stopped at the two red flowers I had been eyeing, and it struck me that despite all of my time wondering about them, I had never investigated them up close. When I touched the petal as I had seen Benoit do, I was surprised to realize that they were plastic flowers flecked in dirt, and up close they didn't actually look real at all. The red petals were synthetic, fading on the edges, and the green stem was made of a hard plastic, like the type of fake flower you would get at Dollarama. They were resilient.

I messaged Maggie back:

> Maggie.
> I'm sorry about your house. It turns out that Lionel won't be coming back to Canada. If you want to stay in his room for a while, you can. Rent is $700. I don't know, it seems a little insane. But I remember once we shared an apple and even though I warned you about the core, when you ate your half you ate the whole thing, which disturbed me a bit at the time, because I was worried that it might puncture your throat or that maybe an apple tree would grow inside of you and burst you open, and I didn't say anything at the time, but in the end, neither of these things happened. I feel hurt about you and Alex, and I'm scared about intimacy between you and me, and between you and Alex, and the whole thing really. And I yelled at a dying man the other day, who both did and didn't deserve it. I guess what I'm saying is that life is complicated, but I'm up for trying something out if you are.
> Love,
> Sophie.

When I sent the message, I felt like an exposed nerve aware of every part of my body, like tiny ribbons of light were dancing all over it, both terrible and vital. The sensation was almost new, but then I recognized something in it elusively familiar, like memory perfume on a stranger walking past. I had felt this way before, I realized. It was like the Big Feeling I had experienced as a child, but without realizing in hindsight it was sexual. Pre-erotic, pre-contextualized, detached from specificity, it was just pure energy. In this way, the feeling tethered itself to everything and nothing. It yawned my body open, reminding it: *You are full of ordinary luck! Don't forget to live!*

Part Three

THEY HAD SHOWN UP AT THE AIRPORT, EACH WITH A little red balloon, like two little emoji people, and the balloons were for me. They were standing apart from each other, a body apart, as if to invite me into the space, as if a spectre of me was already there, and they were holding the place for the real thing. Or maybe I was just jet-lagged, and was hoping for that.

Alex looked the same, dark hair down in the eyes, wearing a big red shirt and his brown jacket from Kensington market. Maggie looked pale but awake and lovely, wearing a black crop top, low baggy jeans with a men's belt, and a red jean jacket. Alex and Maggie hugged me lightly and carefully, like they were hugging the air around me. Perhaps if they could hug that air as a test and feel the energy that I was conveying, they could safely understand if I, too, wanted to be held by them. I did. Or, at least, the air around me did. My glass stuff was being shipped back and I didn't have to worry about it, so we walked to the express train that went from the airport to the subway station near my apartment. Maggie took me by the hand and pulled me ahead, and Alex took my suitcase. While we were waiting for the train, Alex pulled a flossing stick out of his pocket and started flossing his teeth with it. This was a feature of Alex, an unacknowledged split that defined him. Surely the coat was dirty, and he had never washed it, even after buying it. And surely there was dirt in the pocket, perhaps the skin dust of someone long dead, yet he was unbothered by these realities while he poked the pointed object through his teeth to clean them. Some part of his mind knew that the stick was dirtier than his mouth, and some part of his mind knew that the stick was intended for cleaning his mouth, and those parts walked politely past each other in his brain, not minding.

The silence between us felt powerful and magical, like anything could happen. Who knew what might unfold when we started to talk. I carried the silence with me and felt enveloped by it, safe in the cocoon of it. We rode back like that. There was so much to say. Then again, there was nothing we could really tell each other, nothing of value, that we didn't already know. And many things that it felt like I knew, if I tried to put them into words, I realized that I didn't really know what they were at all.

All three of us came into my apartment, my and Maggie's apartment. She had agreed to move in, and upon entering I realized that all of my plants were dead and that Maggie's room was just all of her things and all of Lionel's things, which was very overcrowded. The long beige hallway, lit blue by twinkle lights and yellow by a candle lamp on the wall, the smell of palo santo incense and shoes, wax and stale sweat. Our rooms were on each end of the small apartment, mine bigger with a mirrored closet and two windows, hers with one window and

a small closet, between us a tiny kitchen, the hallway, a bathroom. Barely enough space for one person. She was kind in
not bringing it up then, the lack of space in her room. With
a glance it seemed like she'd been sleeping on top of three
mattresses and several comforters, like the princess and the
pea. Alex grabbed a bottle of Jameson's from his backpack and
poured us all a glass in my mom's egg cups, ceramic white with
tiny lilies hand-painted on. I sat between them at the kitchen
table and Maggie lit candles. I felt expansive, like I had just
been born.

How was it? said Alex.

I missed you, said Maggie, at the same time.

I took a deep breath, and looked up at the shelf ahead of
me, hung slightly above the kitchen table, which was in the
corner of the kitchen. On it was a black-and-white photo of
my mother from grade two, sitting smugly but joyfully at a
desk and wearing a little knitted sweater with wooden buttons.
She was sitting behind an open book, its pages made to look
nearly empty by the poor quality of the photo. She looked into
the camera without fear, full of kindness, her favourite age. I
caught the light of the candle flickering off of the reflection
on the frame and then saw the reflection of us three in it: me
in between and looking forward, while Maggie and Alex stole
loving glances at one another while I didn't appear to be paying
attention. It struck me that Alex would probably stay here tonight, and maybe the next night, and maybe forever, just down
the hall, sleeping through a closed door. The feeling made me
sick in my heart.

It was a crazy trip, I said. And, in fact, I did a lot of work, a
lot of really good work. And the people of the castle, who were
all elegant geniuses, they absolutely adored what I had made.

They said that it was remarkable, I said, lying. And I had sex
with this really wonderful person named Norbert; he wanted
to take me back to Berlin with him, but I didn't think that was
a good idea, because I had to finish my project here. Otherwise
I would have gone, but anyways Norbert and I had all of this
crazy sex — it was so amazing, like I don't even know, I didn't
even know sex like that existed, and neither did he, I lied. It
was so wonderful. I would probably stay there forever if I could.

That's amazing, said Alex.

Yeah, said Maggie, wow. That's all so exciting; you're a princess from a castle, said Maggie, flopping my ponytail up and
smiling like a mother.

How are you guys? I asked.

Alex said he would rather be a bird than a woman, said
Maggie.

Alex started to laugh but was clearly trying to suppress it.

It's not that I wouldn't want to be a woman, just that it
would be so cool to be a —

He's just saying that, said Maggie, grinning at me sideways.

I'm really broke, said Alex. I need a new job, something
steady. I think I need to get something at a restaurant or somewhere where the tips are good.

I'm broke, too, said Maggie. But don't worry, I've got rent
locked down, ha ha. But outside of that, yeah, it's a bit rough.
But I mean, good, you know. Nice.

Things are mostly nice, said Alex, looking concerned. We,
ah — I missed you. And, yeah, Maggie said she missed you, too.

Yeah, said Maggie. I did miss you.

You guys can have a bunch of the tequila and whiskey above
the fridge, I said. I figured it would be gone, but it's still here.

We don't deserve it, said Alex.

Maggie smiled meekly.

I wanted to come home to real winter, but Toronto was stuck in a perpetual phase outside of seasons, where the snow kept melting, the dirt on the road too frozen to be easily cleaned away. I looked out the kitchen window to the parkette behind our apartment, where people liked to sell drugs and push their babies down the slides. The sun was setting in a way that wasn't golden at all. I drank my straight whiskey down in one go in hopes that it would strip me of my personality and make me a shell, full of space, a place where someone might like to make a home, someone other than me.

It's hard coming back here, I said. Here in this grimy city where things cost too much and there are no seasons anymore. It's not good to be here in this nonspace of the world, this place where everything is quick and dirty and low to the ground.

Yeah, I know what you mean, said Maggie. It's gross here.

I looked down at the table, unable to face Alex or Maggie. They were appeasing me, and it was shrinking them down. I was ruining everything with my presence, making us strangers. I couldn't stop; it was either this sort of thing or silence. I felt a cavern in my heart grow dark and deep and waited for the feeling to subside. Instead, and to my alarm, it grew and grew and swallowed me whole. What were these people doing, turning me into a symbol as I had done to Benoit? Their responses to me were not real, not how they actually felt. I felt like they saw me as a delicate and dirty flower, easy to wilt if they couldn't give it enough light and shade and water. Why couldn't they make me feel good, why did they have to go along with the trash things I was saying as if I was some customer in their lives, some clinical interaction to be dealt with so that they could get back to their day?

It was like at my mother's funeral the last time I had been home, the way I could see people searching their brains for the exact right response to my pained psychobabble, as if there was nothing in them and nothing in me to register at all.

Well then, why are you here? I said to Maggie before I could stop myself. I took the bottle from the table and poured more Jameson's into my cup and lit a cigarette indoors.

What? said Alex.

I'm saying to Maggie, why are you here if you think it's so terrible here? If you agree that it's gross and sad and lifeless here, why are you here?

I didn't say that, said Maggie. I didn't say that exactly.

Don't talk to me like I'm your second cousin who you haven't seen in ten years, okay?

I'm not trying to, said Maggie, looking actually alarmed for once.

Fuck whatever it is you're doing right now, I said. I looked at Maggie and Alex and felt the betrayal of their every decision, like their haircuts and mannerisms and ways of sitting — Alex with his legs crossed and his hands calmly on the table, Maggie with her legs spread open and her elbows on her knees, their stupid jawlines and old perfect clothing, their loose pants and tight belts.

Sophie, said Alex.

I'm just asking you not to treat me like a child or some fucking *stranger*. Like how hard is it to just have a fucking backbone?

I felt my nose run down my lip and onto my chin. Good. I wanted to erase any beauty I had before, any sign of it. I wanted to be completely unlike the two of them, to roll around in my own shit, and look up at them and scream, *See! This is what it comes down to! Don't act surprised!*

They both sat there and looked at me, waiting for the next thing. We sat quietly like that, the grey sky out the window unchanging, as if we were out of time.

Alex put his hand on my shoulder and looked at me.

So what's the vibe? Are you guys in love or what? I asked, looking as deep as I could into Alex's eyes.

Neither of them said anything.

Don't downplay it, I said. Come on.

Are you? I asked again.

Yeah, said Alex. Yeah, we're in love.

Maggie nodded her head up and down gently.

Okay. Thanks. Fucking great. Wish I could help celebrate but I'm really tired. Goodnight, I said, stomping into my room and slamming the door.

I lay flat on my bed and whispered into my pillow, Goodnight, fuckos.

In the morning they made pancakes quietly in the kitchen and knocked to see if I wanted any. I didn't answer, so Alex put a couple of pancakes in a zip-lock baggie for me, flattened the air out of it, and pushed it under the door. A baggie full of pancakes slid quietly into the middle of my room, the steam from their heat fogging the inside of the bag. I picked up the bag and ate one of the pancakes but waited until they left the apartment to leave my room.

I was a big baby like that through the winter, but they didn't go anywhere. We all stayed and sat in the bad feelings like big stupid dumplings in a hot soup. It eventually started to feel worth it, to face the badness we had caused each other for the sake of love. We started to feel like a real family in that way.

❀

When I think of my mother I try and think of what she was like before she was a mother. I think about her as a teenager, with her wit, sitting in the velvet booth at her brother's radio show, and I picture the quiet confidence she always had, not even five feet, jet-black hair, something about her face like a pretty rabbit. I wonder if she knew how beautiful she was, like how I wonder that about Alex and Maggie. I think of her as a woman feeling desire and being desired, trying to carve out her own vibe in it all. Do mothers feel like mothers only the second they become them, or sometimes before, or sometimes never at all?

Alex has thought about mothers conceptually more than most men I know. In our early twenties we went to Memorial, a university in Newfoundland on the east coast, in St. John's, where there is no sunshine and so all of the houses are painted like rainbows. We lived near each other on Prescott Street, a street so steep that walking up it caused you to reach your arms toward your toes like an acrobat. I made a lot of spaghetti, and we had friends named Mary and Josh and Wyatt, and they did things like knit vests and roast chickens and make kombucha and drink a lot and go to shows. It was sort of a hippie-punk overlap, or just a culture where people are young and there's no money. We never had any money.

A lot of the time, we would go on twenty dollars for the whole week, and ten of that was on vodka, split. Alex and I often met up at 1:00 a.m. or so on one of our stoops and smoked and talked late into the night, either about people we were seeing or theorists or books we were reading or grand sweeping things about life. Our conversations grew and became deep and circled back, infusing everything unremarkable in life with meaning and importance. We had made this friend,

Iain, who lived in a house adjacent to mine and was fifteen years older than us. Iain was an academic who had gone and lived in Japan for two years and then had spent an entire year inside exclusively reading novels that he found to be important. Iain, who looked a lot like a tall Joaquin Phoenix, would tell us a lot about these books and living in Japan and being a grown up, and we would give him cigarettes, and it would all feel very important. He reminded me a bit of Alex's dad. I seldom did speedy drugs because I was worried about my heart all the time, but the way those chats would fill me up by two or three in the morning was like drugs, my fingertips vibrating with possibility, and the feeling was so generative and infectious that somehow it made it so we never ran out of things to say. I always crawled into my bed late at night with this feeling, like I could split the world open, or condense all of the greatness of my life into one little orb and hold it in my hands, hold it close to my heart.

During that time, when we got really drunk a lot, Alex talked a lot about what he thought it might be like to be a mother, not a father but a mother, specifically. It was always this vibe centred on accepting his mother's leaving based on the fact that it's really impossible to stay a mother for some people because it's impossible to be yourself when you have a title like that. The more Iain got into the philosophical — Kantian ethics, Lacan's psychoanalysis, et cetera, the harder Alex latched on, as if clinical theories gave him further reason to believe that feeling had no right getting in the way of reason.

If she — Alex's mother — was a liberated woman, but there was no space in her when imprisoned by the set-up of the nuclear family to survive within, then what could she do? What options did she really have?

Alex would say things like this only late at night and when drunk, only after we talked to Iain, swaying forward up the street to home, grief loose in the body like dancing, loose like spit.

When we were twenty-two, Alex went away to study in Montreal for almost a year but came back for my birthday, which is April eleventh. On my birthday there was a blackout, which was typical, and it was basically still winter. I turned twenty-three, and we went to karaoke with our friends and stayed late and sang Destiny's Child songs to the room. Later that night, we went to an after-party at Alex's friend Kyekue's house and talked late into the night in the living room, sitting on a futon, passing a cigarette back and forth. Alex and I stayed up so late, all sweaty and leaning into each other, and he kept giving me a warm glassy look, and when everyone went to bed, he smacked the top of my baseball cap and I tickled him, and we held each other by the armpits in the strange light and looked at each other, and he said, I like your haircut, it's really perfect for you, and I said, Thanks, you can have it, and he kissed me and we started to fool around. No sex. I arbitrarily wouldn't let Alex put his hand inside me, just on the outside, and I stroked him between his jeans and underwear, and he was skinny and his hair fell down into his eyes, and he looked at me and said, Sophie, I really love you. I really love you, Sophie, and I said, I love you, too, Alex. And Alex said, Sophie, I love you, over and over, and I laughed a little, really happy about it and worried about ruining it. And in the morning he left and went back to Montreal, and texted me, saying, We are turkeys, and I said, Ya, and felt nothing but a giggling feeling in my lower stomach, and then when he moved back for real he moved into this mansion belonging to a Russian sculptor who

was away most of the year, and by then I was seeing Bobby, and
so we stopped being turkeys for a bit, but I stayed over late a lot
in the winter, and we lit the fire and sat around the haunting
Russian sculptures and listened to modern classical music and
the Durutti Column and drew little pictures with charcoal and
recited essays aloud on topics like Love, and Trust, and Dying.

I think I meant so much to Alex because I took the place
of his most formative woman, and I was there when she disappeared. I carried the torch of his ideas about life and death
and everything, held him when he was sad, held his secrets
somewhere deep where they still sit.

In a way, I get why his mother wasn't ready for some title
that encapsulates so much. I mean, how are you supposed to
be a real person with all of that? How are you supposed to be a
real person when you're also supposed to be the woman inside
of someone else's mind?

They were like otters floating in the yellow kelp. They were
like June bugs, murmurations, midnight park boom boxes.
They had the sheen of the pool during summer pool hopping,
blue with something golden in there, frenetic and undisclosed.
They operated on a strange wavelength of beacons and sounds.
When I overheard them speaking, everything felt gestural, like
they were holding the subject of their interest by making a net
of meaning around it. It took them three hours to play a game
of pool because they were both so bad at it. They lifted each
other's arms up from behind in the streets, spat at each other,
and laughed. Their love was as esoteric and singular as I had
anticipated, and, as everyone's love is, something that I had

no way of really interpreting, whole corners of it I had no real access to, lit upon only by them.

But then there were also difficult things. Maggie pushed Alex to say things he didn't always want to say, to compliment her or be histrionic when it wasn't in his nature, and Alex's lack of reaction when Maggie asked questions or said something funny really annoyed her. Alone and with me it was mostly okay, but in public things weren't always pretty. Their love didn't translate to the public so well. Maggie got jealous, or Alex got annoyed, or Alex got jealous (something I had never really seen of him) and masked it as quiet indifference. Maggie mostly enjoyed Alex's opaque and playful way of speaking around subjects but not when he did it to her and then was direct and complimentary to a different person in front of her.

Alex had been working on an independent film that summer for money. When the film was finished, there was a big wrap party on Toronto Island, which was themed "birds" for some reason that I did not understand. It was at the intersection of the nude section of the beach and the clothed section, so that people had options. People could bring whoever they wanted, because the beach went on and on. Alex went early to help set up, and Maggie and I spent the afternoon in the apartment getting ready.

Maggie mostly resisted talking about Alex to me, which I appreciated. She had tested the water lightly in certain moments, but I usually ended up being unhelpful, either evading her questions or defending him. I thought about how it must be weird for her, to be close to someone who had so many answers to Alex without being able to really ask.

I want to peacock tonight, said Maggie. That girl, Marissa, is going to be there. And Alex keeps saying how great she is, and they've been working on this film, you know, which is intimate, I guess.

I took a sip of wine and looked in the mirror in my bedroom. I had just gotten my hair done, and as a surprise my hairdresser had dyed my hair a sort of strawberry blond colour and given me a sixties shag/mullet cut, which at first I didn't like, but it was growing on me.

Alex isn't going to, like, he's not into Marissa or whatever, I said to Maggie. He's obsessed with you, I said. Which I knew to be true, though I didn't really have access to Alex's thoughts. Surely Maggie assumed we were still telling each other everything, but the truth that I didn't want to entirely reveal was that Alex and I seldom had ever had that brand of closeness, he wasn't one to really divulge; I had never talked about him and other girls or anything like that in a real way, and since I had been back we had forged intimacy mainly through his gratitude over the fact that I continued to show indirect modes of affection, the affection being specifically the act of not asking him anything direct at all. It wasn't that I hadn't wanted to, but over the years I learned that this was an impossible way to get close to him, that he would do things in his own time.

Thanks, said Maggie. Film is weird. Imagine working in a medium where you have to rely on so many other people toward a result, and most often if any element in that result doesn't work, the whole thing sucks.

I think it's about money, I said. It seems easy enough with money.

I just hate film people.

You hate when people have ideas about things.

I hate when ideas lie dormant.

Film is a good way to rouse up ideas, isn't it?

I hate it when people have culturally fixed ideas that are calcified and not their own, and they stick to them like God. And I hate when people ask me what I'm working on. At film things and art things, everyone is always asking each other what they're working on. It's like, fuck *off*, said Maggie.

I think it's just a way of being like, *How are you?*

Well, just ask *that* then. It's so pretentious. Like, sorry I didn't fucking win a Sobey Art Award this year. SORRY, Colin.

Who is Colin, I asked.

No one, said Maggie. Just an annoying name.

I looked on Facebook and realized that my ex from Newfoundland, Bobby, was in town. His band was playing the next night at Burdock, and he had sent me a message: Hey Sophie! I'm in town for a couple of days if you want to hang. I know it's been a while but it would be really nice to see you.

I quickly responded without thinking too much. I told him about the party on the island and that he was welcome to come if he wanted to.

I had decided that I would dress like a big egg, which was vaguely bird-themed. I had made a papier mâché egg costume over the past week and was now putting on the finishing touches of glitter with a small paintbrush. Maggie dressed like a true bird of paradise, tight black jean shorts and a long draping navy silk shirt with bright yellow eyeliner and black lipstick. I wore a white bathing suit under my costume, and black leather boots, and a high ponytail. I would be an egg with a bird inside, not yet born.

Maggie and I biked to the waterfront and boarded the boat to the island as the sun started to set. A bunch of children were on the boat so it felt like we were heading to the New World. We shared a little bit of mushrooms and giggled, giving the kids adult names like Sir Richard Lemanche and Penelope Hucklebee. The air was hot, and I turned off my phone, not wanting to check to see if Bobby would respond. I didn't want to be someone who checked their phone on this night, or thought about all of the possible repercussions of living. I wanted to be dumb and pure in my glitter egg, which chafed around the thighs and immediately lost its shape once I sat down on the wooden pew of the boat. It was sort of a sexy costume, because the egg shape was quite small, kind of an equivalent to wearing a backpack on your torso as a costume. I didn't tell Maggie about Bobby.

When we arrived, there was loud music playing, and about twenty people on the beach, and three big bird floaties out in the shallow water, and a fire. Alex ran toward us in slow motion wearing a bird mask, a bucking silhouette against the orange city skyline. He took both of our hands in his and bowed so low that his mask reached the ground. Alex ushered us over to the fire and introduced us to his film people: Brian, Vex, Zekkia, Marissa, and some other people whose names I immediately forgot. Brian, who wore overalls with no shirt, mesh wings, and red lipstick, had written the script for the movie.

Are there birds in the movie? I asked Brian.

Brian searched the large pocket of his overalls and found a cigarette, put it in his mouth, and lit it before answering me. Then, on the inhale, he said, No, why would there be?

Well, the theme of the party, I said.

That's something different, said Marissa, gesturing warmly to Alex, like they were all in on something.

It's not a weird thing to ask, said Maggie. Sophie didn't ask
a weird thing.

I didn't say it was weird, said Marissa.

Does anyone want to go swimming? asked Alex, grabbing
Maggie's shoulders and looking at me.

Zekkia, the actual art director of the film, turned her back
to Alex and started talking to Vex about certain final aesthetic
choices in the film.

We can fix that in post, she kept saying.

I immediately felt overwhelmed, remembering why I didn't
really like big group dynamics. I always felt like a sponge when
there were a lot of people, accidentally absorbing everyone's
mood at once, and the idea of conflict between Maggie and
Marissa raised the hairs on the back of my neck. I thought
about how I hadn't had sex in a long time and was hoping that
Bobby would show up to break that spell. We hadn't spoken
in years, and for all I knew he was married now with dozens of
tiny wiry farm children with giant eyes.

I had a moment of intense anxiety at the prospect of Bobby,
the fear of letting my hopes float up as they had been, and
quickly turned my phone back on to message him and tell him
not to come, but when I looked at Facebook chat, he had responded two hours earlier: That sounds really fun, do you mind
if I bring my bandmate? We'll come around 9. I don't have
phone data still, ha ha, so I'll just find you there I guess.

It was too late. It was 8:30 and the mushrooms were creating little worlds on the insides of my eyelids so that every time
I closed my eyes I saw the faint image of hundreds of squid,
multiplying. I opened my eyes, and the sheen of the setting sun
on the water was almost too lovely to bear, little ripples bobbing
around innocently. Alex was in the water doing flips.

I overheard Marissa ask Maggie, What are you working on? The sound of the question struck fear in my heart. I got up, slid out of my egg, and ran into the water.

In the water, I stayed several yards away from Alex for Maggie's sake. I knew she wasn't going to get into the water, too. Alex floated closer and splashed me.

Alex, I said.

Yes, my peach.

Bobby is coming.

What the heck!

Bobby is coming to the party, Alex. I feel stupid.

Bobby sucks.

He doesn't suck probably, I said. That was forever ago.

He splashed me, and we floated away from each other for a moment, then back.

Do you think it'll be okay? he asked.

I don't know, I said, looking at him closely.

He closed his mouth and made a tight, goofy smile that didn't reach his eyes.

You look sort of sad, I said, unable to help it.

Sophie, okay.

I'm a little bit on mushrooms, I said.

Cute, said Alex.

Alex, I said.

What?

Okay, I said, defeated.

I looked at Alex and spun in a circle in the water, fanning my hands out to make a circle wave on the surface.

Sophie, said Alex, appearing to hold his breath.

Then I went under the water and once I rose to the surface, played dead man's float. I lay like that for a long time, putting my head to the side every now and then for air. I wondered, If Bobby showed up and saw me like that, would he try and rescue me? When I tried to picture it, the images in my mind contorted, and I could only picture Maggie doing it, running into the water, unable to swim, really. I knew, thinking of it, that Maggie would do that; she would come rescue me from the water if she had to, even if she couldn't swim, no matter if anyone could see her or not.

This struck me as a quiet contract between women.

The water beamed strings of moonlight into my eyelashes and I had a mushrooms thought, full of real truth, about this weird mystery that a professor said in class once, something she had asked me. It was crazy to think about, because what had happened in class was that she, the professor Shannon Culler, had misheard a statement that I had made in class as something deeply profound. I can't remember what I had said, but it was in a post-structuralist poetics class where we were talking about Jacques Derrida, the Derridian return, where repetition leaves a trace, and returning to that same spot is not a true reenactment, not a moment to be lived again, but a moment where you revisit the trace of your last visit, and each time you return there is another trace, so the more often you return, the more traces exist of you in that space but the further you get from the initial experience.

In the class, Shannon, our beautiful genius professor who I was sort of obsessed with, repeated back to me what she had thought she had heard me say. The sentence she said was this:

"Do you think that with this in mind, return is parroting on the brink of address?"

In the moment, when she asked if that was what I had said, I just said no and couldn't really relate to the excitement it was causing her, and there was a flurry of confusion where I really wanted to understand what she meant but couldn't, and then someone else raised their hand and the moment passed.

But in *this* moment, looking up to the sky, on mushrooms, I realized that whatever I had said, she had heard as "parrot," a bird who mimics without comprehension but for the comprehension of its teacher, and that to parrot, to mimic without comprehension for the sake of another, was instinctive in return, that when you came back and repeated something it moved away from what it was to what it could be for someone else, losing its charge to you, like how Knausgaard talks about the distance between feeling and knowledge, that once you know something intimately, once you are given the space to interpret it and put it in your mind in such a way as to call it knowing, the charge of feeling goes away.

This is perhaps one of the reasons people want children, to parrot on the brink of address, to get close to the source of a twofold experience, what you already know too well to feel and what you once felt too intimately to be able to glean clinical information on — revisiting that space and showing it to a mini you, a favourite swimming spot or a storybook or how to tie a knot.

Eventually, I lifted my head up and opened my eyes. It was getting a little colder out and Alex was out of the water, sitting by Maggie at the fire. I peed uneventfully in the water, felt a ring of heat wrap around me, waded back to shore, dried off, and put my egg back on.

❄

By nine the sun had started going down, and people were filling up our marked beach area. I thought of how it would look
from an airplane, just a tiny collection of energy expanding
and building around one set point. I was a bit drunk on tequila
and a little high on the mushrooms but not too much, sitting
quietly and listening to two people talk about Bernie Sanders
and the difficulties of organizing democratic socialism, when
I looked up and saw Bobby and his bandmate Zak walking
toward me.

Bobby's tiny frame and loose blond curly hair and big green
eyes were all the same as usual; his style was a beach-adjacent
style, not board shorts but tapered and wind-worn art boy
pants that looked like they had been pulled out of the ocean, a
threadbare long-sleeved waffle shirt. His genre, if he had one,
was a "synth elf," the type of person who somehow can build
a house with their bare hands but is also very well versed in
electronic music production and can fashion a theremin out of
things lying around the house.

How are you? asked Bobby, pulling a little metal flask out
of his floppy backpack, pushing the hair off his forehead with
the open palm of his hand. He offered the flask to me, and then
when I took it he put his arms around me in a hug, so I tried
to take a sip from the flask with my arm that was now hooked
around his neck, and the flask hit my lip, a warm penny-tasting
ripple of blood filling my mouth that I tried to ignore.

I'm okay, I said. I'm good! How are you?

I'm really tired, he said. We just got back from Berlin,
where we were recording for two weeks, and before that a huge
tour in all of eastern Europe. I feel like a puppet.

You don't look like a puppet, I said.

How does a puppet look, asked Zak.

I don't know, I said, throwing my hands into the air, wanting desperately for Zak to go away.

What are you? Are you an egg? asked Zak.

I'm a real girl, I said.

Bobby looked basically the same as always, though I had barely seen him since my mom had died. If I had seen him at all in that time, that time that was a blur of our breakup and the funeral and the strangeness of interacting with my father through those encounters and the will and everything else, I had confused the memory, had nothing in my mind of some in-between Bobby, just a before and an after, a good Bobby and then a terrible one, though no real event of his doing changed my perception from one to the other, at least nothing I could remember directly. And here he was, post-revoked, to be renewed, maybe. The thought made me dizzy. With his quiet arrogance and beauty he walked to the firepit and sat near it, face and hands into the light, not looking back to see if I would come. Looking at him there was like noticing a muscle in your body only the second it starts to hurt.

Everyone was a bird through the night, and I was an egg drinking tequila. I thought of that Mary Oliver line, "Don't bother me, I've just been born." That's how I felt toward other people. People besides Bobby. Anything new or aging about Bobby, his darkening tooth or his slight crow's feet or his turns of phrase that struck me as unlike anything he used to say doubled back in my mind, like seeing a subtitled movie where you understand both languages and try and reconcile the poetic gap between the two, moving an old language into a new one. My idea of him didn't want to land so I pictured us having sex.

This is the sex, I thought, that I want to have in life, in this current life at this current moment. I tried to remember, in recent years, why I felt so strongly about our relationship, which was mostly difficult, while it was happening.

Talking to him at the fire surrounded by birds, I remembered: it was all of the sex.

Democratic socialism is our only way to win, said Bobby, because it overrides the sentimentality of the Left that often requires a certain form of empathy and sameness that isn't possible among a diverse political party. If people can agree on things that don't risk their feelings and lean exclusively into unsentimental but effective ideas, like taxing the rich and promoting free health care, then it would be easier, but all of this solidarity gets tied up with empathy, and that empathy creates tension when people united under one ideology don't experience life in the same ways, or have the same identity politics.

I thought about a Jia Tolentino essay I'd read recently in her book *Trick Mirror*, where she talks about how the internet has created a culture of neoliberal-tailored individuality that confuses empathy with sameness, the result being that now people think that identity politics means you can't empathize with someone unless you have their specific racial and socioeconomic background, an idea which is fundamentally damning to the Left because it disguises itself as being woke while insidiously making it impossible to unite the disenfranchised and their allies under one front, a numbers game that the Democratic Party needs in order to succeed. I explained this briefly to Bobby, and a light went off in his eyes that brought me right back to when we were close, when he celebrated me for being smart but then seemed not to like me at all if I, say, slept in or watched anything on Netflix.

We held eyes for a moment. I glanced over and saw Alex and Maggie, both dressed as birds, swaying in full wingspan under the light of the moon, near the sound system that was playing techno.

Remember when we used to have sex in the bathtub in the middle of the day, I said, drunk, tracing my finger along Bobby's knee. And then we would drain the water out of the tub and stay, cold, in the tub, until we both came?

He cross-scanned my eyes and said, I remember staying in there for hours on rainy days and bruising our knees, not being able to explain the bruises to other people.

Yeah, we were like, Ohh, I guess I tripped, ha ha, I said. It's funny to think about.

You haven't changed, said Bobby, and though he said it warmly, it stung.

We sat quiet for a while, our knees touching. Then I overheard Maggie's voice cut through the crowd like a caterwaul. I looked up and she was talking to Marissa, leaning toward her in a predatory stance.

You're sorry that HAPPENED to me, said Maggie, over and over. You're sorry that HAPPENED to me? It didn't fucking HAPPEN to me, okay. It was a thing, it was a part of my LIFE!

I tried to listen but Bobby started to wax political again. I drowned him out and heard a name, Trace Ryan, this guy who had been friends with Maggie's estranged brother and who had dated her and who then, around the time her brother had a psychotic break, turned against Maggie and pushed her down a flight of stairs. It was something Maggie had told me about, but she told me so soon after we met late at night, and I didn't know her well enough then to ask the right questions.

Now Marissa was trying to engage, had heard about it from other people.

It didn't fucking HAPPEN to me, okay? My life isn't just something that HAPPENS to me — I fucking have a SAY in my life. I'm not a fucking LOSER. My DADDY doesn't pay for my fucking tuITion! Life doesn't just HAPPEN to people. Maggie spat at Marissa, a foot away from her, standing on the sand. Maggie's arms draped out like she might take flight.

Marissa cowered back, looked at Maggie with the distance of judgment. The music continued, but many people quieted their talking and watched the fight. I could tell people were smirking and laughing about Maggie, the way she was being feral and plate-throwey. I would have felt that way, too, maybe, before knowing her. But she had taught me that WASPy politeness shouldn't be prioritized over realness.

Do you know her, asked Bobby, squinting his eyes.

She's my best friend, I said.

I watched Alex standing, brows furrowed up like accents, trying to figure out what to do. He clearly wanted to interject but was scared. I watched Maggie get close to Marissa, leaning in. Marissa played victim, appearing overwhelmed and unprepared for conflict, looking around to her friends as if for help and assurance, but she didn't back down.

Wow, the rumours are true, said Marissa. Trace was right, you're a crazy fucking bitch.

Maggie stood there, her tooth snarled, blue eyes glinting in the sun, hands up in front of her but open. She was harmless; she wasn't going to hurt anyone, not really, she wouldn't say something like that.

Marissa was the dangerous one. It was clear to me then but maybe not to anyone else.

For a lot of life I had, without realizing it, valued systems that prioritize people like Marissa, polite people, people who could keep it together by making others feel inferior. People who hadn't really had a hard time and who made a show of those who did act up emotionally. But now I knew that was fucked up.

Then Marissa threw herself at Maggie with force, her arms flailing like a muppet. I ran over and pulled them apart; everyone was drunk. I pulled Maggie away from Marissa. Marissa took it as a sign that she had won, smirked at her friends, looked back at Maggie.

You're a fucking beast, she said to Maggie.

I looked at Marissa, her expensive art-girl accessories and her narrow frame and the way her bird makeup glistened and her white silk tank fell off her shoulders in effortless rich-girl luxury.

Grow up, I said to Marissa, who just laughed and raised her eyebrows.

I pulled Maggie away from the water, and Marissa screamed at us, *You're just jealous that I have a real connection with your boyfriend and you know that I could have him if I wanted to!*

We kept walking toward the bushes, and Maggie started to cry, wailing to the moon. Alex and Bobby followed us. We walked the trail away from the beach in darkness, back to the park area full of green grass and trees. We sat in a circle and I pressed my hands against Maggie's face and cheeks. Alex took her hand. Bobby sat there quietly.

Hey, said Alex to Maggie in a voice he'd used with me, the word starting on a higher pitch and then lowering. Hey, hey, it's okay.

Alex knew that words were only partly about meaning and mostly about intention and sound. He cooed at her for a while, using meaningless words to fill the action.

After a while, Maggie started narrating what had happened to Alex in a way that seemed private, though Bobby and I were there, too. It was eleven o'clock, and the last ferry left at midnight.

I looked at Bobby, and we decided to give them some time, so we got up. As we walked I realized I couldn't really rest my arms against my body, and my egg costume puffed out like an egg does, and I had to hold my arms out slightly away from my body, like when you push your arms against the inside of a door frame for many seconds and then step away from the frame, allowing them to float up magically.

Tell me about her, Bobby said.

That's Maggie, I said. We dated for a bit, but now she's dating Alex.

Wow, okay.

Yeah, it's weird. But it's okay.

Is it?

I don't know, probably.

What's she about, what's her deal?

Are you in love with her or something? I asked, feeling annoyed.

No, said Bobby. I just hope she's okay.

She's brilliant, I said, meaning it. She's the best person.

It's good to see you, said Bobby, looking at me with the arrogance of someone who never feels anxious.

It's good to see you, too, I said, but it's weird. It's weird to see you.

You're sparkly like I remember. I was wondering, though, why your shirt felt so itchy.

It's papier mâché.

Cool, said Bobby, turning toward me. He did a thing I forgot that he used to do, which is that he took my hand and twisted his own hand around it, like he was examining my hand, measuring its thickness. Then he put my hand on his neck and kissed me.

We had sex under a tree in a dark corner of Toronto Island, away from the trails. When he went inside of me I felt like I was out of questions for the world, and in that moment I understood his confident, calm way. What would anyone even want to know if they were filled in this way? My back pressed against the tree, scraping, held up, the pulse of us extending outward. He was essentially soft inside of me for a while though it still felt good, until all at once he got really hard and pulled out, came onto my stomach, saying my name, *Sophie Sophie Sophie*, three times over, like a spell.

Then he curved his hand into a rose shape and slid it inside of me, holding me up under the tree so I arched my back, knowing exactly how much of me to fill. He kept his thumb out, circling on the outside while going deep and holding me up, staring me in the eye, the green glint of his irises clear in the half-light.

When it was over he kept his hand in me as if for safety, renewing so much of what I'd revoked. There are different types of safeties, the safeness of closeness and that of distance. They mean different things. We sat quietly for a moment, and then Bobby sat with his legs crossed in the grass facing me, gathered my hair behind my ears, and put it back in a ponytail.

You have to marry me now, I said.

Bobby laughed, his hands shaking slightly.

You can't just be with someone for so long, and then we break up and then nothing for years, and then you reemerge and put their hair in a goddamn ponytail like that, I said. What are you trying to do, are you a monster?

That was really nice, said Bobby. I'm happy we got to do that. I've been thinking about doing that with you again for a long time.

Bobby enveloped me in his tiny body and said, The sex has always been so good like that. It was never not good, you know?

Make an honest woman of me, I said.

We got back to Maggie and Alex just in time to catch the ferry back to Toronto. Maggie was still sort of wasted and exhausted, and Alex looked thoughtful and sad. On the boat back we watched the lights of the city get closer, and I leaned into Bobby. A Dua Lipa song came on in the distance, and Alex got up and did a little dance number, spinning around in circles on the boat, though the boat was half full of drunk people and bicycles. I caught him laugh and then look back to see if Maggie saw him, but Maggie had her eyes closed.

I remembered Alex in the middle of the dance floor almost ten years prior, that night on Halloween when I'd wanted to freeze him in place, felt the vulnerability of leaving his side when I knew he would go on to forge intimacy with someone else, as I had. I had started making out with Maeve on the dance floor; she was dressed as a sexy dalmatian. I thrust my sweaty hips into her, aware of Alex on the periphery, and felt really awake. He saw it all, some invisible golden thread between us; I moved into Maeve through the awareness, channelling Alex. It was a moment like a piece of electricity, palmed.

Then he turned away and I felt it dim. I watched him dance after that, luring people in with a playful whimsy but no real intention. Like it was all in him, an embodied joy, not for on-lookers, not for anyone else.

As Alex danced on the boat, I noticed him looking to Maggie, her eyes closed. His face fell, his movements limped, and I saw then for the first time that maybe it wasn't all for him. That he needed to be witnessed, too, that he couldn't generate it all on his own.

My head felt swimmy, and Bobby leaned his shoulder on me, and the boat — both sheltered and unguarded by the night's breeze — reminded me that I couldn't always tell the difference between inside and outside, that sometimes the boundary dissolved and one became the other, and the skyline became the city became the water, and Bobby became enemy then lover then passive observer, and Alex looked at me with something like remorse, and in a moment I saw that maybe he'd never thought about it, that in getting with Maggie he was giving something between us up, too, and maybe that meant something to him.

And as the boat docked, Alex gave me some sort of quick and brutal look, the kind of look you give when something in your life, at a distance, moves itself out of the pure energy of feeling into the lonely vault of understanding.

After that night, Maggie felt withdrawn and stopped drinking for the rest of the summer. Bobby went back to Newfoundland and we loosely agreed to keep in touch. I waited three days in successful and monk-like silence and then caved, sending

Bobby a three-page-long Facebook message detailing all of the times we ever had sex that I could remember. He left me on "read."

Alex finished his film and started doing community arts jobs, which mainly consisted of him dressing up as mascots at kid events or building sets for off-off-off-Broadway plays.

I started a glass project mosaicking a bathroom at a rich woman named Lillian's house in North York. Lillian, a woman in her sixties with four cats, was seldom around, but when she was we drank wine together. She sat on the toilet, and I felt her eyes on me as I worked. I sanded glass over the bathtub and kept the door closed so that the cats stayed out. When I'd glued everything, I grouted it white, and it looked beautiful, so many different marbled slices of glass in abstract patterns along the wall. The pay was good, and on the last night Lillian thanked me with a tenderness that stemmed from our temporary companionship. I told Lillian about Bobby, and she said that it wasn't about him but what he stood for: a return to the past, to a different time that I didn't have that much access to anymore.

The sky got really pink at night, and flowers hung heavy and low. Sunflowers were everywhere, and when I saw them in the streets I found them to be really scary, like viscerally jarring, and when I looked into their faces I felt like I was being swallowed up, like if I looked too closely I would cease to exist.

But from far away they looked really great, as nice as something you would see on a postcard.

Sometimes I liked to lie awake at night and drink a lot and seek courage to read my mom's journals. I've mentioned this, but also there's another part I liked to do, except maybe it's not that I liked it, but that's where my mind decided to go. The other part is, after letting the sad feeling fill up the spot under my ribs and leaden my arms and legs and the pulse in my temples, I lay there and thought about what it would have been like if I had had the time to be there for her, if her death hadn't been a quick shock but something slow but inevitable, like so many deaths. I thought about that scenario with a painful desire, envisioning myself as a stronger person than I was in real life.

In my head, in this version, I move back to Corner Brook once I hear of her illness, and I get my own apartment, even though I know I will be likely living with her most of the time. My apartment is one small room in an old Victorian house with a fireplace, and I put almost nothing inside of the room, just some candles and books, an abstract stained glass piece in the window, some essential oils, art supplies. In this version of life, I spend my days by her side, looking into her eyes in a way I never could when everything was okay, a way that I never could when things seemed normal. In this version, I stay and take care of her, am protected from the lull of the town the way that really important things protect you from mundanities. I wake up early, hike the Man in the Mountain trail each day, come back sweating, spend the day with my mother, pick up food for us, learn to take care of her the way she took care of me. I hold her head in my lap, and we watch *Breakfast at Tiffany's* on Netflix. I make sure to put a cloth on her head at night when she is scared and in pain, and I hold her bony little hand and feel tender and true.

When I think about this time that I didn't get, it hurts more than anything else hurts, because it is as imaginable as it is impossible and there's no getting out of it, the space between the feeling of inevitability and impossibility.

I don't know what to compare the feeling to, and it's unlike any other feeling I've ever had. If I could guess that it's like anything, I would say it's like wanting so badly to bear a child, only to find out one day that you can't. You can't hold the person you love most inside your womb, even though for so long you were certain that you would, even though for so long it was all you had been basing your life's purpose on, all you had been working toward.

Maggie liked to talk about her favourite bad things to imagine.

So here's the scenario, she said, splaying her long legs in the bright green grass of Christie Pits Park, light through the trees painting our bodies. Alex held her feet, crossing them one over the other, moving them through the light and shade.

The scenario is that you're trapped somewhere, like you're in prison. You're in a cell by yourself. And you have to answer one question. It's a simple enough question, like who wrote "Come on Eileen" or something, and you get as many opportunities to answer the question as you want, and you know that if you answer it correctly, you will be free. But the THING IS: you literally have absolutely no clue what the answer is. Like, it's not something you once knew and need to remember, but something you have truly never known, and it's more than one word. Maybe it's not even a word that you've ever heard before, maybe a word in a different language, or a place you've literally never heard of.

I put my vape between my lips and inhaled, the little crackle of the device if you inhale deeply enough like the sound of wood fire, a weird feature. I was trying to quit smoking.

How many guesses do you think it would take someone to come up with Kevin Rowland and Dexys Midnight Runners? asked Alex.

See, that's the thing, Maggie said. There's no way! There's no way you would ever come up with that. The only possible way being that it's a sort of hangman-type situation, so that if you use a word or say a word, then that one gets included into the final result, but that's not part of the whole thing. But the fact that you get endless guesses, I mean, how would you be able to give up hope when you know the answer is out there?

I thought about what Maggie was saying.

I don't like it, I said. I don't like the idea of the game. It makes my soul feel itchy. No closure.

How long do you think you would try and guess for, before giving up? asked Maggie.

Alex and I both paused and answered at the same time.

Twenty years, said Alex.

I said a month or two. They both looked at me.

What? A month or two, that's a pretty long time, I said.

That's depressing, said Alex.

Typical Aries, said Maggie.

Twenty years is fucked, I said to Alex.

What about you, I asked Maggie.

Oh, I really don't know, she said, throwing her arms up into the air. I wish I had those sorts of answers, she added.

Then Maggie took a knife out of her bag and started cutting up a watermelon. See, I would have cut half the watermelon into even slices, put the other half away. But Maggie went to town on the watermelon, hacked it up into juicy chunks, then jabbed at those chunks to break them in half. She kept cutting the watermelon until the whole thing was just this wet, pink, partly translucent mountain sort of spilling off the plate and into the grass, slow juice rolling down her elbows.

She balanced the plate on her head and said, Hey. Look. She looked at us in a very serious way, trying not to move.

A little kid came running over to us, a little boy maybe two or three years old, chubby little arms and legs, a blue knitted shirt, and a big dirty face bright like the sun.

Do you know what's the best? he asked us.

I saw his parents, tiny figures in the distance, waving their arms. One of them yelled out, "Evan!" but quietly, like if Evan didn't hear them all bets would be off and he would be ours to keep.

What's the best — is it you? You're the best? asked Maggie, smiling.

No, said Evan. Everyone. Everyone is the best! he said, and then hobbled away toward his parents.

Everyone's the best, said Maggie, clapping her hands together. That's really fucking NICE!

Eventually Alex left for work, and Maggie asked me to come to Shoppers and to Starbucks. I followed her like a dog to our bikes and only realized once we were riding that I didn't know why she needed me to come with her.

Maggie, why are we going there! I yelled ahead.

I need to pick up some stuff! she yelled back.

What do you need?

I can't hear you!

But I knew she could hear me.

We stopped at Shoppers first. A small dog, the size of a bag of chips, yapped up at us as we attached our bikes to the same pole that was encircled by the dog's leash. The dog's barking was loud and offensive, its volume passing the threshold of what feels okay for ears. I looked at the dog and opened my hand, reached my arm out toward it like I was casting a spell or like Matilda moving something off of Miss Trunchbull's desk with the power of her mind. The dog continued to bark the same way, maybe louder, and I remembered that I had no power. Maggie returned and then took my hand, and we crossed the road to Starbucks.

Let's get pumpkin spice lattes, said Maggie, growing manic, almost like drunk Maggie, though she hadn't been drinking since the beach incident. *Maybe she's getting cabin fever with all of the sobriety*, I thought, but then she pulled me past the cash register to the back of the store.

I need you to wait out here, she said. I'm going to pee.

Aren't we going to get PSLs?

In a bit.

You're being annoying, I started to say, but looked at her and saw an urgency in her that I didn't want to combat.

I waited outside the door for what felt like hours. I heard the sound of something being ripped in the bathroom, a click. People came to try and wait in line, and I raised my eyebrows at them, suggesting with my face something along the lines of *trust me, you don't want to go in there*, just so they'd go somewhere else.

Maggie opened the door and pulled me in, and I knew instantly that something was about to happen. The space we were in felt starkly unreal and new; I saw the bathroom — once a drab and terrible windowless room, maroon and brown and grey — as suddenly a room of importance, the site where one moment could be swallowed by the next giant moment that would change all future moments in a big way. The unintimidating roundness of the dirty white sink, lit like a stage, reminded me of the Colosseum. Maggie held her hands behind her back and looked at me in a way that I knew I couldn't ask her what was up, there was no point; she would decide when she wanted to tell me what she had to tell me.

Parts of the room seemed to separate in this anticipation, become something else, not defamiliarized exactly but like each element of the room alighted under the sheen of strangeness; the water dripping in the tap, I remembered, was a life source, the substance we needed most, and the paint on the walls was made of pigment that came from something real and true, like a flower.

Maggie got close to me and bit her lip. I tried to match my breathing to hers while I waited for something to happen. Inhale, exhale. I looked at her lip and realized that if other people saw us, it would look like we were about to kiss.

She revealed what was behind her back: a pregnancy test with pee on it. Before it did anything else, it made me think for a moment of my cup of pee from the Big Feeling, in all of its secret glory.

Maggie, I said. Fuck.

I tasted blood and realized that I was sucking inwards inside of my own mouth, drawing blood from my gums. The metallic taste sat in the back of my throat as Maggie's information tried to dawn on me, though when I searched for a feeling mostly all I could pin down was nausea.

Is it Alex's? I asked. Part of me didn't believe that it could be, like pregnancy was some faraway thing that my friends and I were incapable of achieving.

Do you want to do one, too? The pack comes with more than one.

I'm good, I said, looking at the pack, which appeared to have a sale sticker changing the price from $23.99, slashed out in red marker, to $21.99.

She saw me looking.

I think it's fine to get the on-sale one, she said flatly.

Are you sure this is the type of thing you want to cheap out on?

It doesn't really matter anyways, she said. I already did four of them last week, and they all came back as positive, so …

Baby.

She broke, ripped off her black hoodie, and hunched in the corner, hands through hair.

I didn't try for it, she said through sobs.

It's okay, I said.

I told him, she said. I thought I knew. I said I would do another one to be sure, a few days later.

It's okay.

He's going to go for a bit, she said.

What do you mean?

He said he needs to go for a bit, she said, the sentence breaking like glass. To get money. He didn't explain it yet. But that's what he said.

He'll come back, though, I said, reaching down for her, trying to get her up.

Later that night, from my room, I heard Maggie come out, sobbing in the hall, and Alex descending the stairs. Then Alex underneath us, his steps vibrating. I looked out the window to him opening the gate.

I opened the door to Maggie crying on the floor in the hall. Her orange silk long-sleeved shirt was wrinkled and wet around the sleeves.

He's going to B.C. to plant trees. For three months, to *get us money* or whatever. That's what he said. He said he's like, in. But. I thought he meant for a week or two. To clear his head or ask a relative. I didn't ... not like that.

Maggie's voice broke, and then she slid her back down the wall to the floor. Through sobs, she said, I just ... don't know ... if he's actually ... going to come BACK.

Sure he will come back, of course he will, I said to her. But I really didn't know what he would do.

I *did* know, though, truer than anything, that he wasn't going to B.C. That just wasn't something he would do.

I tried to think of what he might actually be doing, and the only thing that made any sense was that he would be going back to Newfoundland for some reason, to try and find his mom maybe, or to ask his dad for advice. Maybe he wanted some closure, or guidance, or money. I wasn't sure, but it almost seemed to me like the B.C. thing was what he decided to say because he wanted me to know he was lying; we always made fun of people who went tree planting. It seemed like, even if on a subconscious level, he wanted me to know that something else was going on so that I could decide whether or not to be there for him, or at least so that I could know something that he didn't want to say out loud.

Maggie draped her arms around me, and we synced our breathing together in the dimly lit hallway, feeling the strange quiet of Alex's absence. Maggie cried onto my shoulder, the heft and release of her sobs like an ocean I remembered.

Can you, she started to ask, and stopped.

Then it was quiet again for a long while but for our breathing.

Do you think you could be, whether he goes or not, could you, she started again. I just think, I don't know if this really makes any sense without you. And Alex wants ... and I think I need you, too, but if you don't ...

Of course I can, I said.

After an eternity, I made Maggie peppermint tea and we went to her room, where I tucked her in and turned off the lamp. Something in her face calmed in the seconds before I turned off the light.

Maybe we all need more mothers than we have.

Maybe we all need as many mothers as we can get.

A child is like a thought, until it's nothing like a thought at all. You make a decision long before it's something other than a thought, and that's the part I don't understand. Like death, a new life is something that doesn't easily turn itself around, taking so much with it. There are so many reasons not to have a child — the end of the world, money, the fact that they take up every ounce of your time and heart — but people still choose to do it, and even when they don't choose, it still happens very often, something like half the time.

Growing up, I had never asked Alex about it. And then, once Maggie told him, we had one really brief conversation before he left, where he told me that he had always wanted a child; it had never been a question in his mind.

I've always had a feeling, he said. A big, beautiful space like the sun, bright and impossible to look at or ignore.

He looked at me and started shaking me by the arms and making a glugging sound, smiling wide.

Do you want to have that feeling, I asked him, and his face darkened for a moment, then came back alit.

Well, when she told me, once I had a moment to think about it, some space in me got all full and bright. Like she put a cherry pie in there. Like she filled it with fireflies.

I thought about this, Alex's Big Feeling. Growing up, I had brought him into my Big Feeling with the idea that everyone's was the same, that it was something he would surely feel in the same way with the same connotations. But when I thought of the feeling, the filling up had to do with something entirely other than a different life. It had to do with my own life, and sex, and art, and connection. Although the feeling was quelled for a while when I kissed someone whose lips I really wanted to touch with my own, the feeling also revealed itself in moments where two things that seemed deeply disconnected found a way to come together, or when things seemed to line themselves up, despite the odds.

Alex left three weeks after he told Maggie that he was going. He said he wouldn't be able to communicate much because of tree planting, being "in the bush," but he would be able to call maybe once a week. The last time we saw him before he left he wouldn't look me in the eye because he knew that I knew he was lying. I had always found him to be a bad liar, but seeing him lie to Maggie I realized that he was actually not so bad at it, except for the fact that he gave more details than he would if he wasn't lying. When Maggie asked him what he was going to pack, he talked for about forty minutes about all of the things you need to bring with you tree planting, whereas I knew that if he had actually been doing that, he would have answered in a succinct and joking way. When he called once a week on the phone, it sounded staticky, which Maggie also seemed to believe, though I knew that he was definitely just taking a candy wrapper and rustling it up against the receiver, which is something that I had taught him to do when we were, like, fifteen after watching *The Parent Trap*.

Maggie and I joined a water aerobics class together at the YMCA on Dovercourt and College. On Tuesday and Friday mornings, we would get up early, bike down to the gym, put on our bathing suits, and slide into the cold bleachy water, where a toned and pimpled teenage boy named Cameron would teach us, some old people, and apparent moms how to shuffle our bodies around effectively. I think Maggie wanted to do it to be around other moms mainly, plus she had quit smoking, which she said was making her feel like a serial killer.

When we did exercises involving jumping, Maggie held her stomach with her open hands, even though her stomach was mostly flat still. Other women looked at her and nodded knowingly, and she smiled back in a private, shy way that also had the air of campiness she always had, that quality where you didn't know if she was letting you in on the joke or not, but it somehow didn't matter, you wanted to be there anyways. I wore a navy blue Speedo racing suit, blue goggles, and an orange swim cap from the days I used to swim in a more serious way. Maggie wore a red, frilly one-piece that was like a bikini but connected at one part on her torso. All of the strings and ruffles on the bathing suit took her forever to sort out in the morning, and she adjusted the suit a lot while we were in class, too.

There were lots of babies at the YMCA, baby fitness culture, babies doing yoga, and babies playing basketball, and babies drinking smoothies. It made me realize that I had known babies in Newfoundland but none in Toronto, not really. Most of my friends were approximately twenty-seven in Toronto and lived paycheque to paycheque, which was Maggie's case, too, but as you can imagine not always the most ideal scenario to be bringing another person into.

It's hard to explain, but the pregnancy, even early like that, changed Maggie, changed her on the level of energy and aura. Whereas before she had seemed so energized and feral, now she seemed calm and specific, like she had given herself a context. I kept waiting for her to have some big moment and start freaking out, but she seemed to grow calmer and happier about her situation as time went on, integrating the baby into conversation in natural, playful ways.

I just hope it doesn't turn out to be some little fuckboy, she said once, walking home from water aerobics. It seems like millennials all misuse therapy talk, so I wonder what this newer generation will be like. I feel like it'll be a boy, but I doubt gender will matter by then, by the time it's old enough to pick its gender.

Are you scared? I asked, as Maggie wrapped a scarf around her wet hair. It was getting colder out.

Yeah, I mean, for sure. And I don't think I'll be able to send money to my dad anymore, because it will probably be hard with money stuff, even though Alex is making money now.

This statement sent a wave of nausea through me, reminding me of Alex's lie. I didn't know for sure, not 100 percent, that he was lying. Like I didn't have real proof, but I could just feel it in my bones. What would happen when Alex came back without any money at all? Had he thought that through?

What about besides money? I asked Maggie. Does it scare you, the idea of another person?

She linked my arm and leaned her head into mine and thought about the question.

No, she answered eventually. Growing up, my family was always on top of each other; at one point we all shared one room, and things were claustrophobic and intense. And it's weird, but I miss that in a way. I miss that sort of messy intimacy.

I don't really get that, I said. I never had that.

I think it's good to have lots of people, when there's a lot of love, said Maggie. I think it's scarier when you give all of your love to one person. Because then if something happens and for some reason you have to stop, then what are you supposed to do? Where are you supposed to put all of it?

Though I knew she was getting through everything, I could hear Maggie crying at night most nights. I knew she wanted me to hear her because she left her door open enough that I obviously would. The sound made me want to cry, too. She sat cross-legged on her bed in her messy room that looked like it belonged to a child, laptop on her knee like it usually was, the blue glow of the screen lighting up her faerie boy–like features, making her eyes so blue that they seemed full of lasers. The first couple of nights like this, I just sat at the edge of her bed and told her it would be okay, but on the fifth night she pulled me close, and I spooned her from behind, which made her cry harder than ever and then stop crying entirely. I flattened her hair to her sweaty head and tried to understand her like my mother had understood me, tried to sponge all of her context and her pain and her beauty and her real lived moments and thoughts so that I could be someone comforting her who really *knew* her in a forever way.

One night, I showed her the song "Sawdust and Diamonds," by Joanna Newsom, the most soulful song to me. We listened in silence, lying flat on our backs in my room with the pink light bulb plugged in, plus candles. The song moved me every time I listened to it, made something quake inside of me. I tried not to listen to it too often, scared that I might ruin it. Maggie listened politely in silence and then when it ended asked if she could put on the song she liked.

Sure, I said. But what did you think of my song?

Uhm, I don't know. There's a lot of breathing in it, her voice is really squeaky.

But the *words*, Maggie.

She pursed her lips together and put on "Don't Make Me Over," by Dionne Warwick. I listened and it didn't do much for me.

This song is for me what that song is for you, I think, she said.

But she has so much composure in that song, I said. There's nothing quivering in there, she's not risking anything.

Vulnerability through composure risks a lot actually, said Maggie.

Why?

Because it's riskier to be wrong when you say you're definitely right than it is to be wrong when you admit all along that you're maybe being wrong.

I thought about this for a moment.

Why do you want to have a baby with Alex?

I want to have a baby with you and Alex, she said.

Don't you think it's a little crazy, I asked, feeling the gamble of the question sit in my throat. I had had an abortion once and remembered that the thought never crossed my mind, the thought to not have an abortion.

She moved her gaze from the ceiling to my cheek, which I could feel but didn't have it in me to look back.

I don't know, maybe, said Maggie, her voice smaller and less sure than I expected it to be. I can't explain it. Like, obviously I'm pro-choice, but when I found out, it was like I couldn't even think about any alternative, like not doing it was like breathing in really deeply and deciding not to exhale. I don't know.

I hear you, I said. It's not unheard of. I mean, we don't really have any money, and it feels like we're all really young, but I guess we're not. I guess we're almost thirty and lots of people have babies then, and it's not some crazy thing, not really. It just seems that way. Or it seems sort of impossible, but I guess things seem impossible, and then they happen and they become part of the fabric of existen—

I just worry, Maggie cut in, talking really quickly. I worry that, like, you and Alex have this context and this life and this world, and I just come into it and everything happens, and sometimes I think you must hate me. Like, I couldn't say it before, because I fear the power of suggestion, but like, I find it really remarkable that you're here in the way that you are and that you want to be. And I want to honour your and Alex's relationship in whatever way you want me to, like if you guys want to have sex —

LOL, I don't think that's a good idea, I said. And I don't want to have sex with Alex at this point. That would be bonkers. And that's fine, I said, suddenly feeling more stern than normal, like her broaching all of these things that were, of course, difficult finally gave me the opportunity to confront them and her.

Though I didn't feel mad.

I just feel like you and Alex have this shiny, beautiful energy together but also individually, said Maggie. And I want to be like that, too, but I can only be the way I am, and I know it's whatever, but I really, I really have a lot of love. And I love you, and I love Alex, and I know I'm sort of messy and broke, but I really will love this baby so much. I already love it so much that it makes me want to die, she said.

Don't die, I said. Plus, you're remarkable. You're really special. You do something special to Alex, and to me, too. We love you. I love you so much.

I love you, too, she said.

I already loved the baby, too. Or at least I loved the idea. But that's what always happens. You fall in love with the idea, and then, if you're lucky, you learn to love the person, too.

Part Four

FOUR WEEKS AFTER ALEX LEFT, I BOOKED A FLIGHT TO
Newfoundland for the following week on Air Miles, using
Reward Miles. It was cheapest to fly into and out of St. John's,
which meant that I would arrive and then take the DRL-LR
bus across the province.

The DRL bus takes fourteen hours each day to cross
Newfoundland, and it stops twenty-five times along the way,
finishing its westbound journey around 11:00 p.m. at an Esso
on the highway. DRL coach is the only way to get across the
province without a car, and it is owned by a Pentecostal family
who choose the day's entertainment. There are nine small televisions screwed into the carpeted ceiling of the bus, which
screen back-to-back G-rated VHS tapes rented from the gas
station at the Port aux Basques ferryboat dock.

There's a way that the ground looks from an airplane that
I'm happy to have missed, because this time there was a lot
of fog, luckily. The thing I was number one scared about

seeing coming in was that familiar but distant expanse of land below, out the window, the little cars mathematically gliding along at consistent speed, little pools of water shining black and surrounded by green, but most of all the part right before the landing part, where you're flying over the ocean for so long and then suddenly the island appears as if out of nowhere or out of luck.

The part where the water meets the land was always something that made me feel sad as a kid, spreading the message through my mind and heart that no matter what you do or what you amount to, the world is much too big and random to really honour your exit in a way that matters. It must have been sort of annoying, having a kid so worried about death, like a small dog barking bloody murder at the door every time the wind blows. But my mom never seemed to mind and always got me to draw puppets on the barf bags when we started our descent. The flight attendant would ask me to put my tray up, and I would put it up, and as soon as they walked past, my mom would say, It's okay, you can take the tray down, it's not going to hurt anyone. So I would pull it down again and start drawing again, until a flight attendant came back to remind me again, getting more annoyed each time.

I used to think that my mom did that, the hand puppet distraction, because she wanted me to be distracted by an obvious activity. But then, when I went to university and came back once for Christmas and mentioned it, she said that she was so adamant about the puppet drawing thing because she knew the only way that I would stop worrying about an all-consuming, impossible anxiety was by putting a manageable one in front of me: the anxiety of knowing that the flight attendant was going to come back again and again and get sort of annoyed.

About ten percent of your attention was on the drawing part, she said. The other ninety was you constantly using your peripheral vision to see if anyone would catch you pulling the tray down again.

I think that you have to really understand someone to be able to do something like that.

It made me feel really lonely, the idea of feeling so small in relation to the vastness of the world while looking out the airplane window, paired with the memory of my mom and then the added reality that there wasn't anyone who would distract me like that anymore, and I didn't feel like I could really do it for myself. I thought about the baby that Maggie and Alex were having, the baby that Maggie wanted to be my baby, too. I hadn't been able to picture it in Toronto, but with a little distance I could think about it more concretely and for the first time realized that it would become a big human one day, one who probably looked half like Maggie and half like Alex, and that human would maybe one day be on an airplane by themselves, too, maybe even after the rest of us were dead. What would that human make of everything, looking back, and would I provide them any comfort? Would we be able to mean a lot to each other, not despite but because of our confusing roles to each other, the fact that I was neither a mother nor a father but someone simply there and loving, the fact that they weren't technically my child but someone I was predisposed to love and spend a lot of time with? It scared me to think about too closely, but the fear wasn't the type to make me want to run — it had nearly the opposite effect: it was scary because there was something confining in it, being in part responsible for a life, but I knew if I were to turn away, turn away from Maggie and Alex and the new person, then

wherever I went there would be this spectre of difficult love
and the "what if," the regret of not having been there, would
be impossible to move past.

The number for Alex's father, Robert Delaney's landline, was
written in the front of each of my journals spanning from 2000
to 2006, which I kept in my bedroom closet in Toronto. Most
of the journals from that time start with important phone
numbers and birthdays, then get into detailed descriptions of
all of my likes and dislikes, and then finally take on an apolo-
getic tone, vis-à-vis me not being able to write often enough,
fearing the building sadness caused by neglecting the book or
maybe its reader, with a sort of business-casual tone, like "Dear
journal, hey! Excited to catch up, sorry I have been absent these
last weeks. It has been a really busy time what with school
starting again, I'll get back to you by Monday at the latest."
After a few apologies, I would start to resent the journal, deciding that it was being too demanding, and then I would stop
writing entirely.

The funny thing is, while with most notebooks I would use
the blank pages for other drawings or whatever, in my specific
journals I wouldn't touch the sacred white pages, but instead I
had to leave them blank to keep the journal's hopes up. In one
journal, I drew a little happy face on each blank page following
the final apology, to keep the journal company, because I knew
secretly that I wouldn't come back.

Would Alex come back?

I didn't like to consider this, whether Alex would come
back. Because I knew there was something in him that didn't

want to, that would want to run, not just because of his mom but because there's always something running in Alex: running away from a serious question with a joke, or from conflict with a whistle, or from hurtfulness with a sometimes-passive kindness. There was something at once active and inert in him, like he constantly wanted to circle the centre, flirt with it, but never plunge himself fully in. This quality made him special and beautiful and himself, and he wouldn't be Alex without it. But it also possibly had the ability, in all of its reach, to make him do something unforgivable, like leave Maggie and me.

Was Alex a good man, one of the best I had ever met? Or would the qualities that made him magical to me also make him bad, bad in the worst, most insidious way? It was weird to think about how the same person could be both, the same person could be the best person I had ever met or the worst. The astounding weirdness of that was not that opposites exist in a given person but that surely the feelings were all tangled up inside of him, and so one decision (to do a good thing, or to do a bad thing) was not very far away from the other decision, was probably right next to it, breathing into its ear.

I went to Corner Brook first because that's where Alex and I grew up and that's where Robert Delaney was, even though Alex and I lived in St. John's when we were older and spent more time together as adults in St. John's. It was the hardest to go to Corner Brook, because that's where everything happened, and the last time I had been there was for my mom's funeral, and I never wanted to go back, and I had told myself that I wouldn't go back, not until I was a beautiful and strong person who was also an adult and had a real life, not when I was some lone, confused person like now.

Dad said I could stay at the house, which he still owned, though he was usually in London, Ontario, these days. It was the house I grew up in from birth until I moved out, and it seemed like when I got back to Corner Brook, a mill town of twenty thousand people, I would either need to stay there, or I would need to not stay. I told Dad I would water the plants, though, at least. He told me where the key was hidden. It was in the mailbox in an envelope that said "key," he told me, which I thought was sort of disconcerting considering the fact that he left for weeks or months at a time, and there were many valuable things inside.

First I called Robert Delaney late at night the week before I came home, because I knew he would be into the Black Horse then, hopefully loose enough to reveal some info about Alex's whereabouts. I called him at 1:00 a.m. Toronto time, 2:30 in Newfoundland.

While the phone rang, a funny thing happened — a montage of Robert appeared in my mind. It was not a montage of experiences I've had that involved Robert but, rather, a collection of things in my mind that he had potentially done in our long absence from one another: Robert buying a one-litre 2 percent Brookfield milk and Canadian Classics regular from the convenience store up the hill from his house, asking for a bag even though the smokes went into his pocket, his rough left hand grasping the handles of the grey, wet plastic bag and wrapping it around his knuckles, swaying the milk side to side as he skulked home. Robert looking handsome in his scary way, a friendly giant, his face with twice the number of features as normal people. Robert walking to Casual Jack's, on West Street, and sitting at the bar, quiet and warm and troubled, frenetic, falling in love with women who looked like they had an ounce of mysticism in them — a long earring, a loose pant — too quickly asking for their time of birth, specific in his tastes but always trying to channel them through the vague sensibility of a small town in order to combat the lonely alternative of eternal solitude. His inability to leave the city, how he was committed to waiting for her, Alex's mother, even once that possibility disappeared entirely.

Am I in love with Alex's dad, Robert Delaney? my mind asked itself.

Then my mind quickly responded: *No.*

Then I thought about Bobby, the time he went down on me in the bathroom at Rocket Bakery while an all-ages show happened in the main room, the sink running, and then after, dripping lazily once he turned it off.

Oh, I thought, and then Robert Delaney picked up.

Hello?

Hello, Robert Delaney? Hi, this is Sophie. Um, Alex's ... Hi, sorry it's late.

Sophie! Hello, my little tulip, so lovely to hear your wind chime of a voice this hour of the godforsaken night. I can see the moon from my window, and I'm picturing your face in it right now, just glowing down through my telephone line.

I could hear Robert Delaney rustling with the telephone cord nervously, could picture his giant hand making an ivy tendril of it. His voice was round and smooth and hollowed out. He was appealing to me in a way where he was also sort of revolting at the same time, and that feeling made the allure of him feel all tangled up, though beyond that I wouldn't be able to really explain it.

Robert, hi, yes, it's nice to hear your voice, too. I'm calling about Alex ...

What have you been up to, my dear? I was going to write you and ask if you could make me a little glass piece, a little something to hold the light. The light isn't right these days. It seems to have nowhere to land, I'm afraid. And I was thinking maybe if you made something with a warm orange hue, maybe an abstract piece, smaller than my window, I could do a reading for you. I was going to see when you were coming home next, or back I should say, not home. Or whatever you would like to call it …

I would love to make you a thingie, Robert, but I need to talk to you about Alex. It is very important. I need you to tell me if he's there or not, because I'm coming there, and I have to find him and talk to him about —

You know that I don't get between these things. Alex is an adult man, my darling, I can't involve myself in his relationships, my dear, even for someone as sparkly as you, said Robert, now sounding very tired. He had been on some other side of this type of conversation, looking for Alex's mom, calling whomever, and it got him nowhere. Something distant, I could hear, had calcified in his voice, a taut quality that insinuated that he could never do the world the favours he had asked so fully of it and for so long. It wasn't personal, he was just the wrong person to ask.

But if you're coming to town I'd love to see you, he went on. I could make you a cup of tea and look at your chart, or we could both do a handstand and summon the little Whitney ghost from the basement — she's still here, I promise you.

Robert, that would be lovely except I am coming all this way, and I don't want to do it if I don't even know if Alex is there. Can you at least tell me if he's on the island? I'm not going to kidnap him. I just need to talk.

Go on, responded Robert Delaney, which in Newfoundland means stop.

Robert liked to evade things the same way Alex did. He was just illustrating the point of my fear about Alex, how certain qualities can be perfectly charming and loveable, but the same ones can be infuriating when there are real stakes, like someone complimenting your bracelet right after you get hit by a bus.

I'll be there in a week, I said. I'll be there on October fifteenth, and I'm going to come visit you, and we're going to talk, okay?

Looking forward to it, my love, said Robert.

I got into Corner Brook around 11:00 p.m., and decided to walk from the bus stop to Dad's house. I only had a big backpack, and though the walk was partly on a wide stretch of depressing highway, it was only about one kilometre or so and didn't take long if you could find somewhere safe to cross the road. I walked past a section of the golf course and remembered as teenagers going in the wooded areas there with Alex and a boyfriend I had had named Scottie, where we would make little huts that were collapsible so that no one would find us out, and we would drink in the huts and smoke cigarettes and listen to Radiohead quietly through a portable speaker and talk.

It seemed okay to be there, more okay than I thought it would seem. Dad was still in Ontario with his girlfriend. I avoided the street that my mom's apartment was on even though it was the quickest way to get to where I was going. Instead, I walked up a steep road that my friend Sylvia used to live on. Corner Brook is like a big bowl, the centre of it its lowest point, and everything sort of inclines around it. It's not really the type of town you can bike in, but it sprawls too much for walking, and while some areas are cute and have trees and are cozy and human-like, it is easy to stumble into a really depressing dead zone, like the highway road, where suddenly all the joy is sucked out of whatever you are doing, and you instead have to focus on not getting sprayed by slush or falling into a ditch on the side of the road.

It was getting chilly and seemed like it had already snowed once or twice, and the air had a cold blueness to it, even though it was only fall. I tried to see everything through the cozy lens of nostalgia, walking past a park where I spent so much time growing up. Margaret Bowater Park meant a lot of things, because my mom brought me there when I was a baby, but also I went there as a teenager to go swimming and drink and smoke weed. The patch of green and the hill and swing set and trail that lead into all of the twists and turns and unknown spaces that had been so exciting to me at one point made the boring area glow with reverse potential, like moving out of an apartment and then getting a good look at it once it's empty and sparkling clean. I felt like I could keep a handle on everything, myself and life and the purpose of the trip and being okay, as long as I let the cozy associations to space and objects sit at the forefront of my mind and not sink in too deeply, as long as I could not think too hard about them.

Going into the house was really weird, though. There was no note because Dad didn't know before going to Ontario that I would be coming. Mostly things were the same, the dining room to the right of the entrance with an out-of-tune, old upright piano and too many prints on the walls and plants that were growing crispy and brown from neglect. I turned on the lights and realized that Dad had replaced all of the warm light bulbs with fluorescent ones that gave a garish, depressing sheen to everything, so I quickly turned them off. Mostly the fridge was full of condiments and different types of expired milk and cream. I found a can of tomato soup in the cupboard and heated it up alongside some Ritz crackers. The crackers were soft and stale and had probably been there for years. I found some cheese in the fridge that seemed fine and cut off some little cubes and dropped them in the soup. I remembered that this had been one of my favourite things to eat as a kid, but I hadn't had it in years for some reason.

The house was eerily quiet because the town was eerily quiet; there was no cushioning the silence with the sound of traffic or someone screaming in the distance like in Toronto. I brought the soup into the living room and realized that a lot of the stuff remained — wooden cabinets with floral tempered glass and matching bookshelves, dark green walls and large poorly made oil paintings by friends of my mom who had been going through art school and giving her their messy test pieces, photos of me growing up and photos of all of us, spooky colour-corrected photos from the early twentieth century of relatives who looked like ghosts and dolls. The liquor cabinet was still full of random stuff; Dad didn't really drink. But Dad had replaced the nice white delicate sofa and loveseat with big maroon La-Z-Boys that had cupholders in them, making everything in the room look disjointed and weird. There were still things — liquid soap in the bathroom, candles that my dad never lit — that I recognized as things my mom would have bought, and maybe I remembered her buying or interacting with some of them, or maybe my brain was just making that up, filling in the space of nothingness with an explanation.

It's not that I was mad at my dad, not really. I had thought about it, him leaving so late in life, and I knew that my mom asked him to leave. He betrayed her and she wanted out. She wanted to be alone. And she had friends; she was beloved. But maybe I was mad at how unfair it seemed, and maybe I was mad at what it exposed — that you could build a whole life with another person and it all comes crumbling to a halt, and then so soon thereafter you're alone and tragedy strikes and no one is there to help. I didn't like to think about things being as good or as bad as the way that they end, and I knew that life was much more complicated and textured than that. But still, to think of her having to do everything for herself after spending a lifetime doing everything for other people, it seemed wrong to me, like life had no real romance in it beyond the romance one could offer oneself, like there was no underlying order or sense to anything that happened, and things just went on and on in random, disjointed, and sometimes cruel ways.

Maggie and Alex and I were all apart — if you saw us on a map, little flashing lights, we would all be far enough away from each other. Or maybe Alex would be so close, though it didn't really feel like he was. My plan was to talk to Robert, and if Robert didn't give me any clues, to go to St. John's and talk to Alex's aunt Wanda and maybe some of our old mutual friends and try and track him down. It's hard to hide in a city where everyone gets off on each other's business. Maggie didn't know why I had come home; I told her that I needed to take care of some stuff at the house for my dad, and I hadn't told her that I hadn't been back since my mom died, so it didn't seem like a big deal, maybe. There was a beat when I told her, like a cold gust of wind, where I saw on her face that she worried that I was leaving, too.

I'll be back in a few days, I said.

And I could see in her face that she wanted something unreasonable of me, or something that she deemed so. She held it back with her eyes even though I tried to say with mine that she didn't need to, that there was no point in her becoming polite all of a sudden.

I went into my old room on the ground floor, which was eerily similar to when I had graduated high school. I had done my first mosaic, which was just with mirror, on my purple wall: a big rose like the rose in *Beauty and the Beast*, made with glass from an Ikea mirror that had broken when I had slammed the door once, the whole mirror sliding quickly to the ground and cracking into intricate lines like a spider's web on the floor. I had painted over the mosaic so it looked like a faint image of a rose jutting out of the wall, but was pretty inconspicuous. It probably would have been a nicer thing to look at if I hadn't painted it, but then I remembered that at the time something felt unfinished about the rose when I was done gluing all of the pieces onto the wall, so painting it over was more for ceremony than anything.

My old room was full of pictures of me and my friends and family, which I realized was not very cool. I hadn't been very cool. I think coolness is something that a person establishes when they're two or three, and if you're not cool by then there's not much you can really do about it. A picture of me in grade two with a mushroom cut and "sideburns," wearing a turtle-neck covered in cats and a little patterned blue kerchief (my mom always added those to my outfits, like I was a small house pet) and blue jeans with clouds on them, smiling widely, half toothless, after completing a scat style a cappella rendition of "Somewhere Over the Rainbow," which I had thought was an excellent performance then and until years later, even though the teacher had to pretend to cough and leave the room while I was performing because she was laughing so hard. People made fun of me for it, and I asked Alex, who said he remembered the performance even though we weren't yet friends, and had found it to be technically bad but overall inspiring.

In one corner of the room there were stacks of boxes that my dad didn't throw away from my mom's old job as an accountant, I'm sure less for sentimental reasons and more because he wasn't sure if he was allowed to or something. There was a bag of gift wrap and a white dresser with a mirror covered in Billabong and Volcom stickers, old books (but shitty books like *Confessions of a Shopaholic*, ones I didn't want to take with me when I left), a bunch of CDs including all of the Alanis Morissette discography, Meat Puppets, Nirvana, Modest Mouse, and *Big Shiny Tunes* 2 through 15. On the wall was a hook full of hemp necklaces that Alex and I had made that didn't sell — most of them had some sort of defect or specificity that made them less marketable, like a Canadian flag bead or a knot at the end that was too small for its loop.

I thought of Instagramming them but then remembered that if Alex saw, it could be a problem. I had tried messaging him since he left, just sending little messages that said, *Alex*, or *Hey dood I wanna talk to you*. But his responses were vague, starting with *Brb* (tree emoji) and slowly becoming nothing at all. If he was looking to find his mom to ask for money, which was possible, then was he actually ready to try and find her? What if she wanted nothing to do with him? What if it really hurt? Would he just have to pick himself up by the bootstraps, find some shitty job in St. John's for two months, and then come back to Toronto pretending everything was fine? It all seemed too much to take on alone.

The hope was that if I found him and gave him a look that said, *You really have to come back, when you're ready*, that he would listen, or at least that was the best chance of him listening.

The quiet in the house slowly filled my heart with a thick, liquidy sadness. It was somehow worse, the fact that things were nearly intact from my mom's touch, than had Dad redecorated completely. Or even if things had stayed exactly the same it would have felt better. They had broken up a couple of years before her death, but still he hadn't changed much. Instead, the details of her warm touch had disappeared slowly, replaced by lifeless substitutes. In the bathroom, my dad had replaced the sweet little hand towels my mom always collected with brown paper towels in a pile, like in a public bathroom. I lit a dust-covered candle in the living room and turned off the fluorescent lights, and I poured up a large glass of Jameson's, toasting quietly to her. Then, remembering that no one was around at all, I started singing "Moon River" and pulled out some old photo albums and some of my mom's notebooks from behind the shelf by the giant flat-screen TV.

I drank and read and looked at the photos for a long time, remembering that my mom had amazing style. Her handwriting had a perfect and curly slant to it, and her clothing was gorgeous — not expensive but really tasteful, simple silks and cotton pieces. The pictures of us as a family when I was little seemed to belong to someone else, like I found them in frames at a yard sale and was intruding by looking upon the images with such attention. I found some Cuban cigars in a box that my dad owned, cut the top off of one, and smoked it, coughing aggressively on the first inhale.

After three Jameson's I felt my head swirl, and a storm collected in my chest. Without seeing it coming, I cried desperately for about half an hour, big heaving sobs that seemed to come from almost nowhere, some depth that I didn't have clear access to. It was weird, but it felt good; it didn't feel desperate. It was a feeling that didn't need anything, didn't have any desire in it, which was odd, because often I missed her so much that my desire to see her again was tangibly painful, like someone was lighting a thousand matches under my skin.

Afterward, I felt tired and walked up to my dad's room to see if any of Mom's old clothing was in her walk-in; she had taken some with her when she moved out, but she had left all the good stuff — power suits from the eighties, long paisley dresses that had fallen out of style and back in. I found the outfit she wore at my christening, a red, black, and purple shirt and matching long skirt with pleats and big wooden buttons. It looked cute and was well made. I sent a picture to Maggie and told her it had been my mom's.

I would literally wear that, said Maggie.

Same, I responded.

Then I found old nighties that my mom had, silk and different soft colours like Easter. I tried some of them on, too, feeling the room spin around me in a pillowy nice way. It didn't feel weird to try on all the clothes, but then again it seemed like all of the crying settled something, like I was powerless, which felt good.

I took a photo in one of the nighties and thought about who I could send it to. Part of me wanted to send it to Alex or Maggie or both of them but it seemed like a bad idea. I decided after a moment to send the photo to Bobby on Facebook, even though he had been very quiet since our last encounter.

To my surprise, he "saw" it right away and messaged me back.

Hot, he said.

Thx, I responded, feeling my hands get sweaty.

How r u.

I'm ok how r u.

Good, have been thinking about u.

I'm actually coming to St. John's in two days, I responded, holding my breath.

Bobby started writing, then stopped. I felt creepy, like Bobby had been with me a lot in recent months, in my fantasies and dreams, but talking to him reminded me that it was possible I had not been in his thoughts at all and that it might be intrusive to keep him there with me in that way.

Then he wrote: I want to c u.

I want to c u too, I responded, and squealed into the quiet room, startling myself.

U can come over, I think u can come over the night u get in. How long are u here for?

Just a couple of days, I said.

U shld come over just wearing that with a coat over it. Or nothing under the coat.

I sent him a kiss emoji and went to pee — now that I had his attention it would be fun to seem a little harder to get, to leave him wanting me, maybe leave him a little confused.

When I came back I said, K, r u still in the same house u were in before?

Ya, just knock. Come by at, like, 10.

Okay, 10 p.m. on Saturday. Got it. See u then.

I waited for a sign off but Bobby didn't respond, and he hadn't "read" my final message. I assumed that he saw it and could read all of it without having to "open" the message and didn't see a point in responding further. It didn't matter — the excitement of the plan made me energized and gleeful enough that I felt like I might explode. Why is it that when a big sad feeling comes in, normal happy feelings are euphoric, relieving in their importance? I pictured Bobby and me walking through the Battery, on the side of the harbour in St. John's, holding hands like when we were younger, the sun setting and the wind blowing in our hair. He would pull a little thing out of his bag like a muffin or a tiny loaf of bread and give me some, and it wouldn't feel like time was really a factor, and it wouldn't feel like anything was going anywhere ever, and it would seem like life was about nothing except sex and touch and wind and it would be easy.

The feeling inspired me.

I got up from the floor, grabbed one of Mom's long wool coats out of the closet, put it on, pulled on some knee-high socks, and wrapped one of Mom's dainty yellow silk scarves around my neck and tied it in a bow. I put on my boots and went outside, not locking the door or bringing a wallet. I walked down Brookfield toward the cemetery, which was not the cemetery she was buried in. I tried to hold my breath walking through the cemetery, gasping for air every ten seconds or so — the cemetery was big and took a while to walk through. I remembered my friend Carl, in high school, whose job was to maintain the grounds at the cemetery but also he rode a unicycle as a form of transportation, so you would always see him unicycling through the cemetery with a rake and shovel poking out of his backpack and his blond curly hair flopping in the wind.

It was too cold to not be wearing pants, but the walk wasn't so long and I was determined and feeling numbed by the whiskey. There were jitters in my chest like hummingbirds, sending me on a mission that felt more important than any mission I had ever been on. Why wait? Why wait until the day, when the night was full of silence and importance? I noticed how some graves had no flowers, some had real ones, and some had plastic flowers that were faded and ripped, and I wondered if the people who brought the fake ones knew that they wouldn't be back for a long time, whereas the people who knew that they would be back brought fresh flowers that they could replace over and over. I cut through the bottom of the cemetery, ran through the empty intersection, no cars to be seen, and started walking through the parkette.

Along East Valley Road was a string of old houses, not so old but classic Newfoundland townhouses, wood and painted exteriors, big windows; you could almost feel the floors creaking inside before you even knocked. Most of the lights were off except in the one I was looking for, where an orange glow sang out through the top-floor window.

I looked up through the window for a few minutes, seeing a figure moving in the distance, backlit, the shadows of the figure growing and shrinking the closer it got to the window. For a moment the figure appeared as Alex, a lanky man with hair cut to just below his big ears, a big nose, and movements that seemed at once spastic and calculated.

But then, as it got closer to the window, growing, the figure became who it always had been outside and inside the magic of wishful thinking: Robert Delaney.

My phone had died, and I didn't realize how late it was until I noticed the clock above Robert's oven, one of those cat clocks with the eyes and the moving tail. The clock said 1:30 a.m.

Is that right? I asked.

I'm not totally positive, my dear. I think it's pretty much right, said Robert. But then again I like to set it a little late so that *I'm* not ever too late, you know what I mean?

Robert reached for my coat and I remembered what I was wearing underneath. I hugged the coat close to me and said I was cold, but after a minute or two I was starting to sweat; the apartment was hot, the wood stove blazing in the corner. Robert's apartment looked like I remembered it but dustier; it looked like the apartment of a reclusive writer, stacks of books piled up, flipped over, splayed open on the floor, really beautiful books that looked expensive, their spines bent beyond repair, lots of wooden furniture, dozens of empty brown beer bottles in the corner, and some midcentury modern, coloured glass kitchenware that would go for one hundred bucks a pop in Toronto but Robert probably got at Salvation Army for two dollars. It was weird, though, because Robert wasn't a writer or an artist of any kind as far as I could tell. Growing up, I remember he had been chipping away at writing some grand thing, something about the philosophy of taste (taste for food, not cultural preference) from a Deleuzian angle, but he was trying to make it really accessible, like Yuval Noah Harari or Slavoj Žižek or something. But he never finished it, even though he worked tirelessly. Alex said that Robert had asked him to read it, and what Alex read seemed thoughtful and heavily researched but "highly unintelligible," like he was dealing in too many ideas at once, and the whole thing was so incoherent that Alex couldn't get through it at all.

It was hard to say where he went from there, but I didn't want to ask.

Sophie, it's such a treat to see you. You're looking great, really glowing. Are you okay?

People don't really say you're looking great and ask if you're okay in the same sentence, I said to Robert in a flirty way. It's important to flirt with people, even if you don't want to have sex with them. It makes them feel the sparkle of eros, and it makes them feel special. Plus it was hard to help it with Robert; he was really charming, a giant version of Alex.

I'm okay, I said. It's weird to be back.

I recognize the coat, he said. That was your mother's coat. You know, if your mother and I had been a bit closer to the same age —

Okay, okay, I said, pressing my feet up near the wood stove as if I wasn't sweating. Robert was about fifteen years younger than my mom, who was forty when I was born.

Robert cracked a beer for me and we cheersed, looking each other intently in the eye. CBC Radio Two was playing quietly in the background, like white noise, which felt like a relief.

How are you? I asked.

Oh you know, things are what they are, he said. The kids are getting into astrology these days. Suddenly everyone knows their rising and everything else, so they're doing most of the work for me. At first I thought it meant I would get less business, but actually I get way more. I mean, there's only so much you can get in a small town, but I've been doing some online stuff, too, am thinking of teaching a class on it. But I gotta be careful if I teach a class. I don't want to put myself out of business too much, ha ha.

I felt the warmth of Robert Delaney's sweet, deep laugh and started to relax. Not thinking, I slipped off my coat and felt the energy shift in the room so slightly, a nearly indescribable shift. I looked up at Robert, whose eyebrows were furrowed, and then down, remembering I was wearing a negligee.

Great.

Sit down, I said to Robert.

Robert sat down on a small kitchen chair next to me. I'd never seen him look scared of me like he did in that moment. I remembered, because of "me too" stuff, that I had more power than normal. Not me, personally, but things had really changed since I last saw him. I would never, but something in him seemed to know that if he so much as looked at me with desire I could really mess up his life. Part of me liked to have that power, but a bigger part of me didn't like to have it, even though I knew I was supposed to like it. He rested his elbows on his knees, sat about three feet away from me, and looked me square in the eye in a very serious way.

I crossed my legs and reached in my pocket for my vape, which of course wasn't there. My mom didn't have a vape; it was her coat. He saw the action and interpreted it, handed me a Pall Mall, and lit it with a match, protecting my face from the initial spark by cupping the smoke with his giant hand.

What do you know? I asked him.

Sophie, my darling, this really isn't —

Do you know Alex is going to be a father? I asked.

I looked him in the eye and saw a sparkle of surprise and melancholy and something else — excitement? — flash over his face. I thought he probably knew, but maybe it was intense to hear it from someone else, to hear it spoken out loud in the actual world.

Congrats to all of you, he said.

It's not my baby, I said.

He looked at me quietly, waiting. Then he laughed.

I guess it sort of is my baby, too. Right. Thank you.

Had Alex explained that to Robert?

Robert, the thing is, I need to make sure Alex is going to come back. I know he said he is, but I feel unsettled, and Maggie feels unsettled. And I feel like we haven't really been able to talk properly or be around each other since he found out, like before he left we didn't really get the chance.

Robert exhaled and lit his own cigarette. Plumes of smoke billowed slowly around his head, like clouds in a dream.

I'll make you a deal, I said. I'll give you Maggie's birth time, so you can do her chart, and maybe that will put you at ease a bit, too, knowing about the person your son is with.

I assume she's got a lot of Pisces and Aries, he said.

It was true.

Robert looked at my face, really looked at it: he looked at my forehead and cheeks and eyes and nose and mouth. He looked really sad, doing it. Then he started laughing again.

Sophie, my sweet, I care deeply about you, you know that. But Alex is my son, and I need to respect —

Robert, come on, I said. I'm so over this. I'm so over this playful, funny whatever it is that you guys do. Like what's so fucking funny? This isn't funny at all, okay? This is real life. Alex's mom LEFT. That was real life. This isn't some fucking game, okay?

I felt the heat rising on my neck and cheeks. I looked Robert in the eye and realized I had lost something, some slow and quiet, playful closeness we had been building in our silence until I flipped out. Maybe having a half-naked, drunk, fevered woman appear in the middle of the night to remind him that his wife had left him wasn't the way into Robert's heart.

He swallowed. I know all of that, Sophie, he said.

Then why won't you help me? Can you at least tell me if you know that Alex is going to come back?

Sophie, my darling, he said. Sophie, my sweet little rose-cheeked tulip, you've always been so fiery in your way. I know you don't think that about yourself, but you have this life in you, this determination that makes people feel safe, because it makes them feel less lost. You've always been able to just make things happen, fearlessly, or if there is fear, it's not as big as whatever counters it. You'll maybe never see it as something good, because it's not very pretty and it's not very gentle, and I know you want to be those things, too. But it's really a beautiful quality, and Alex needs it, and I've always been so happy that you guys have each other. We both admire you so much, you know. Alex used to talk about it all the time, when you came up in conversation, which was often — he got this sparkle in his eye, like the one his mom gave him when he was really little, every time she walked in the door. Anyways, I don't want to cross my wires here or cross your wires, but I want you to know that.

It was weird to hear Robert say all of this stuff. How could I make anyone feel safe and comforted when I didn't feel either of those ways at all? It seemed wrong, like a trick, that he was saying that. Plus, I was obviously full of fear.

Robert inhaled through his nose, and I noticed that the pores on it were bigger and redder than they had been the last time I had seen him. His face was aging, sinking, a calm resulting from something, maybe he had resigned himself to knowing he would never find her now, not really; it was too late. Even though I didn't really believe him, what he told me made me feel good and shy and less powerful than I had felt before he said it.

Why can't you tell me anything, then? I asked. If I'm so important to him and he's so important to me, why can't you tell me where to find him?

Robert softly put his hands on my shoulders and looked me in the eye again. His face had aged, but his eyes were bright green like baby plants and stardust.

Sophie, he said, my dear, at a certain point in your life, in *my* life, well, it's gotten to be quite lonely. And the foundation is shaky at best, I gotta say. And I'm okay, there are things that I find such beauty in. But the stakes are high for me, and I have to be a man of my word. If I start to slip, and if I start saying things I promised I wouldn't say and doing things I promised that I wouldn't do, then I don't know how far I might go. It might not seem like a big deal to you, because you're young and you have so many people. But I can't afford to lose anything else. You'll figure it out with Alex. You'll do the right thing. I trust that you will.

He had made up his mind before I even came in the door.

Robert's giant hands were still on my shoulders. It felt in that moment like we would kiss but that it wouldn't be weird or sexual even though, of course, it would be both of those things in a way, and it would be a small and beautiful moment that could ruin everything, which felt appealing in that moment for some confusing reason. I leaned my head toward him, still feeling drunk. He stood up and pulled me up, too. He was so much taller than me, my eyeline just at the top of his chest.

He slid his hands down to my forearms, closing his long fingers around them. Then he pulled back so that we could really look at each other. All of our words fell cold and soft like snowflakes.

In those seconds the good parts and bad parts of my mind felt so tangled up, like they might overlap and become each other.

Like a psycho, I almost leaned in to kiss Robert Delaney when he instead wrapped his arms around me in a giant hug

and held me like that for a long time. Patchouli, sweat, gaso-
line, cinnamon, peppermint.

We stood there like that for a very, very long time. The hug
made me feel soft and clear-headed, and in the clarity I sort of
wanted to die. Not in any way that would bring me to action,
just that things were exhausting, and there were certain forms
of pain that I felt in my being that no amount of misdirection
or processing seemed to be able to fix. They just sat there in
my body, making my body feel like mud, breath as prayer,
a tunnel, tight pipes, blood, the purple heat of blood, song
drumming in the temples. It would be nice to feel nothing for
a moment instead of always having to feel *some*thing and have
that something be a stand-in for a different something, and on
and on.

I knew Robert Delaney felt this way, too, though knowing
that didn't really help.

The sun started to come up, and neither of us said anything
else and I left, the creaks in the stairs articulating themselves
like half-spoken wishes flung in the cold morning air.

I woke up drenched in sweat on my still-made childhood bed.
The dream was terrible because it was just like real life, except
I couldn't breathe or move at all. She — the figure — was a
presence down by my feet at first, and I could feel her weighing
down on my shins and ankles, like a heavy dog sitting there.
Otherwise things looked the same in the room — the same
tapes on the shelves, the same little pink TV in the corner.
My arms and legs were the same, too, except they weren't really mine because I couldn't move them at all. And then I was

breathing, but even that was like something that had to be fully intentional, something that I had to affect consciously in order to keep it going. She moved up the length of my body, cold and heavy like the worst possible feeling of dread imaginable. I knew her — the Old Hag — she was a mythological creature in Newfoundland and only revealed herself here, because it was here where she lived. Her face was twisted and shadowed, the eyes all green iris with no pupil, but if I looked at them they came at me like a screensaver that zaps you into its endless abyss. She was known for causing sleep paralysis and for assaulting people in their sleep or, in lesser cases, pressing down on people's bodies in nightmares, or sometimes for just sitting at the end of the bed and watching from a distance.

There was no real way to explain the Old Hag away, because people who hadn't known about her would come here and see her in their dreams, only finding out anything about her in their waking life afterward.

I didn't know anyone from Newfoundland who didn't get visited by the Old Hag at least once in their life.

What do you want? I tried to ask her, though no words came out.

Let me go, I tried to say.

Instead she burrowed into all of me, and it was like I could feel the distinct contours of my insides, parts separate from the invasion of another. I tried to thrash around and get her out; she was so expansive inside of me, filling me up so that nothing had room to move. I tried to breathe despite her filling me up, but it was getting harder and harder, like there was nowhere for the air to go. I felt a splitting pain down through the top of my head into my heart and stomach, down my legs. I closed my eyes in the dream and let my mind run in circles, trying to ignore her presence so that I could spin slowly and deeply enough to drift into a newer, safer consciousness. Somehow I got away from her, but it took all of the dream strength I possessed and exhausted my sleeping spirit to the core.

I didn't realize there was so much *space* swimming inside of me when the Old Hag wasn't trying to get in there, such vast interior emptiness. But then when I woke up, that space was all I could feel.

When I awoke, it seemed like it was best to move on, that more answers would await me in St. John's, on the other side of the island. I wanted to stay for another day, but the Old Hag was on to me, and seeing Robert Delaney made me feel like it was hard to stay afloat and that making decisions that weren't hurtful to others was harder, and harder the deeper you went into yourself, if going deeper took you further and further away from the outside world and the consequences of your actions on other people. I had only been gone a couple of days, but it felt like I had left the new part of me in Toronto, and some part of my soul had been waiting for me in Newfoundland, and that part of my soul washed over too big a part of me, such a big part that I didn't even know what other parts there were, or where they were, or how to access them.

I got out of bed drenched in sweat. It was 11:30 a.m. I took a shower in the upstairs bathroom, where there was nothing but green Ivory soap on the shelf. I showered quickly and towel dried my hair with a starchy white towel, feeling like the walls of each room in the house were closing in on me, like I would have to move through each of them quickly in order to escape. It was too lonely and still and sad in there, like nothing else existed and everything was impossibly far away.

I made a gross pod coffee on my dad's coffee machine and looked for something to eat quickly. The bread was mouldy, the fruit was brown and soft, and the milk carton felt ominously heavy, though I don't know why I even lifted it up to check. I found some old dried apricots, a can of tuna, and three granola bars. I opened the tuna, ate half of the can with a fork while drinking the coffee, flushed the rest, cleaned the can in the sink, and packed the rest of the food for the bus ride. I hadn't really unpacked, but the pile of my mom's clothing and possessions were still up on the floor in my dad's room. I ran up there, stuffed a few of the things in my bag, and shoved the rest into the closet downstairs in my old room.

When I left the house, I didn't have long to get to the bus, and the cabs didn't accept debit or credit, just cash, so I had to walk really quickly to the bus stop. I forgot my detour and ended up walking past my mom's old apartment. I was almost beside it when I realized the mistake, and it made me feel sick and breathless.

The awning was a light grey, the windows big and wide open. Inside, it appeared that there were two young boys playing on the sofa, their heads bobbing up over the top of its blue velvet back pressed against the window. The apartment wasn't really big enough for a family, so they probably didn't have any money. It was about the size of my and Maggie's apartment, though. The front still had sections stoned off for tulips and carnations, but it didn't seem like much was growing there, long green weeds bent over the artificial lines separating the grass from the flower beds.

Seeing the apartment was okay at first until I realized something that made the hair stand up on my arms. Out of the corner of my eye, before looking away for good, I saw that the curtains remained, the hand-embroidered white sheer curtains that my mom had made and loved so much, right there in the windows, like it was nothing.

I wanted to run inside and snatch them away, take the curtains back to her. It didn't seem right that these people who didn't even know her and probably didn't even understand or care about the curtains should get to keep them like that, with kids who probably smeared ketchup and dirt on them. I thought about knocking on the door, going inside, and tearing them down and taking them. I knew that was a horrible thing and that actually the family probably did like them and appreciate them, and what business did I have going in and taking something away that now belonged to this young family all piled into one little spot?

I imagined someone coming in and taking something from the baby that Maggie would have, some forks and knives or a towel, and it made me feel defensive and raw. Still, my body, despite itself, started moving toward the door of the apartment.

I reached toward the doorbell, my heart pounding in my ears. There was something growing in me, some velocity that wanted to expand. Maybe it was just the desire to affect something on this trip, the desire to take control over something that I could actually control, something that wasn't my mom being gone or Alex being gone or Maggie being pregnant or Robert Delaney's being lonely or any of our sadness. I wanted to make something really happen for the sake of good triumphing over evil, heroes defeating villains, et cetera.

But when a little boy with dishevelled brown hair and a SpongeBob shirt opened the door, wiped his nose on his forearm, and looked up at me sideways with a really cute, mischievous grin, I felt like a big idiot.

Who is it? someone said in the background. His mother.

She came over to the door and saw me standing there. To my surprise, she was someone I *had* known. Her name was Rebecca and we had been at C.C. Loughlin together, elementary school. She was only a year older than me.

I pressed my toes into the front of my shoes and remembered the bus.

Sophie, she said in a sleepy, weirded-out voice, is that you?

Hi, no. I'm sorry, this is totally the wrong address. I'm sorry, take care. Sorry, bye!

Before she could say anything else, I closed the door and started speed-walking up the road.

Walking the rest of the way to the bus, I wondered who would do such a careless thing, who was in charge of stuff like that at the time? I tried to remember, going back through my memories, a Rolodex of blurry faces and colours and flashes of little scenes from the funeral, like it happened a thousand years ago but also like it was still happening right then and always would be, too many details and names and bits of information to keep up with. I couldn't think of who it might have been, a person in charge of her stuff, in charge of figuring out what to do with it all, with all of my mom's life, the inventory of her existence.

Hours into the bus ride, I awoke from another fevered dream and realized ... maybe *I* had left them there.

❀

Alex's aunt Wanda worked at this second-hand bookshop called Afterwords, in St. John's, and I knew where she lived, too. I had known her a bit growing up, but when Alex and I moved out to St. John's, I saw Wanda more, and she was only about fifteen years older than us, and she was cool, a cool aunt who I sort of considered to be my aunt, too. When Alex and I were in undergrad, she would take care of my cat when I went away sometimes, or bring one casserole for Alex and one for me, and sometimes she took Alex and me out and got us really wasted at one of the Irish pubs on George Street. My favourite memory with Wanda was once when she was going through a breakup with this total loser named Kevin, and she knew that Kevin sucked and that it was over, but she was really depressed about it. That night included our robbing the washing machine in her apartment building (which was close to George Street) for loonies and buying singles off of people in the street and smoking them together, Wanda randomly finding some guy who sold her a single Pall Mall and kissing him on the mouth outside the bar we were going to, ending the night with Alex and I split-sided laughing, watching Wanda sing "Dancing Queen" in a very serious, ominous way at Georgetown Karaoke, a little lodge-like spot that only welcomed bar locals at three or so in the morning.

So Wanda and I were pretty tight, and though we hadn't kept in touch over the last few years, I felt like she might inform me about Alex.

I didn't get into town until about 11, and by the time I checked into my Airbnb it was almost 12:30, so I waited until the next morning to try and find Wanda. My Airbnb was in a defunct hotel called the Franklin, on Water Street, right at the very bottom of the city, downtown by the harbour. It was pretty nice for how cheap it was — an old Victorian hotel with high ceilings and brick walls and big windows — but it was clearly falling apart with no one to put any real maintenance into it, and I'm pretty sure it was haunted, too.

On my way to Afterwords the next day, I saw a few of my old friends, Bobby's friends, Ashley Weatherby and Janette Coleman, walking down Water Street holding hands. The image of them together like that warmed my heart, and seeing someone I knew other than my best friend's dad was such a sweet and tender feeling after these strange and difficult limbo days. Seeing them draw closer, I realized how flayed I felt by being there at all, like I had no context to tether myself and could be rewritten over and over at any moment. I let out a squeal and ran toward them. I was waving frantically, but it strangely seemed like they didn't see me.

Then when I got close enough that there was no way they couldn't hear me calling their names, a sinking feeling took over me. They *could* hear me, but they were trying to avoid me for some reason.

Janette looked up at me while Ashley averted her eyes.

Janette, hey, I said.

Janette smiled tightly and affected an air of politeness that was more cruel than ignoring me completely, which Ashley was doing.

Hey, Sophie, she said.

What's up, I said, feeling sick. I just got to town and —

Sorry, Sophie, we gotta go. Nice to see you, said Janette, and they quickly walked away.

I looked down Water Street, toward all of the cute little rainbow houses and the fog rolling in over the hill and the meadows in the distance and felt it all close in, like in a nightmare. What was going on? Was I a ghost, too? I wondered, or were they mad because I had moved to the mainland? Or maybe they were in a fight and the timing was bad.

I stuck to that idea, that maybe they were in a fight and the timing was bad, and their coldness had nothing to do with me.

I picked up some coffee for me and Wanda, something to give her before I asked her about Alex. It was possible that she wouldn't be at the bookstore, but then, she was one of the only employees there, so if she still worked there, the chances were pretty good.

I got to the dusty window of the store, and a wave of nostalgia washed over me. The store was one of those rooms that feels like it's been itself for so long that you can't imagine anyone actually setting it up, and you can't imagine what it might have looked like empty or what it might ever look like as anything else. The window was full of display books that were to lure customers in: early editions of *To the Lighthouse* and limited issues of Shakespeare and some beautiful Al Pittman books. There were also newly bound books by Gaspereau and Running the Goat, wooden mobiles and dream catchers hanging in the window, along with those little gumdrop gems that take in the light and refract it in rainbows against the wall inside. I looked past the wooden mobile and saw Wanda in there, looking pretty much the same as before: this combo that was common in Newfoundland but one that I seldom saw anywhere else. She was sort of mousy, with stringy, straight, thin hair to her shoulders that walked the line between brown and grey but was more brown than grey.

The combination I'm talking about, if it were to be distilled into two words, would be bookish and hardened. She was thin and wore Sally Ann clothes, grey wool tights, a plaid skirt, and a cashmere, button-down cardigan with a tight lavender Lycra tank top underneath. From afar, you might mistake her for a twenty-year-old precocious arts major, but up close you saw the frown lines in her face, the yellow on her pointer and middle fingers from smoking, the thick eyeliner and push up bra, could sense sandalwood and cigarettes and a bit of halitosis. It made my heart pang for Newfoundland, the only place I had been to where there is enough space and isolation and distance from the world for people to really be themselves without even thinking about what that meant.

When I walked into the store, the door hit a series of wind chimes that resonated through the room, startling Wanda, which I thought was weird considering it surely happened every time anyone came inside. When she looked at me, her face betrayed a second of tenderness and then, just as quickly, hardened completely.

Hey, Wanda, I got you a coffee.

Wanda crossed her arms. Sophie, she said.

Long time no see. Are you still seeing David?

Wanda sized me up head to toe and took a minute before answering, like she was trying to decide which tone to go with.

David took off with some other married woman to the mainland, said Wanda, grinning. But that was over a year ago, she added, scrunching her face and pushing the air around quickly with her hands, shooing, as if David was a tiny fleck of dust in the air that she wanted to get rid of.

Do you have time to take a break? Do you want to go for a smoke with me? I asked her.

Sophie, I can't at the moment. I'm very busy.

I looked around and there was no one in the store.

There's no one in the store, Wanda, I said.

She looked anguished.

Fine, she said.

Wanda and I made small talk and joked around in a way that felt familiar, and I begged her to come for drinks with me when her shift ended at 5:00 p.m. I would have to appeal to something in her to get any information out, I knew, which felt ugly because it felt manipulative, but I didn't see any other options.

We met in a dark bar below my Airbnb, with slot machines glowing close enough that they lit our faces yellow and blue. I knew Wanda would like it there because it was like we were hiding, and everyone in Newfoundland got off on hiding at least a little bit.

A few shots in, I looked Wanda in the eye.

Wanda, now listen, I said, affecting more of my Newfoundland accent than I had done in years. I need you to at least tell me if Alex is here, in town. I need to talk to him, I said.

Wanda bit her bottom lip and looked at me, shaking her head back and forth. A part of me knew that she knew that she was going to tell me something the second she agreed to go for drinks.

Rob called me to tell me you was on your way, she said.

I went to pull out my vape but left it in my pocket, feeling like she would find it to be a stupid mainlander toy and that would make her want to stop telling me anything.

Did he tell you anything else? I asked. Did he tell you that Alex has a baby coming and that I'm not the mom —

You bloody well better not be, four shots gone into ya, smoking like a fucking chimney, she said.

Wanda, I'm just worried that he's here and that he's trying to find his mom, and I know that that's maybe not a bad thing but, like, I know Alex, and when he gets outside of his world or whatever, he's sort of like a dog, you know how he is. And you can train him, and he listens.

Wanda looked past me and her eyes glazed a bit, like she was thinking about something else. I had lost her with the symbolism talk, maybe.

Men *are* like dogs, she said.

I don't mean in a bad way, I started, but then realized maybe this was a good angle.

Fucking stupid little dogs running off, doing whatever it is they want to do, whenever they want to do it, Wanda started.

Exactly, I said, though this was not what I meant at all. If Alex was like a dog then so was I; we were like dogs in the same ways, mostly. Easily broken. I was worried that his mom would reveal something to him if he found her and that that thing, whatever it was, would speak too loudly, would pin him like the Old Hag had pinned me, and maybe it would hurt him, and maybe it would make him want to run even more, or maybe it would break something in him that couldn't afford to be broken when everything felt so precarious.

You know what, Sophie, Alex *is* in town. Or at least he was. I may as well tell ya. You'll find out eventually anyways, people likes to talk. Now you find him and give him a fucking mouthful, you hear me —

What's he doing here? Like, do you know —

Wanda took me by the arms.

Now listen, my dear, she said. I'll tell you something. So Alex's mother, she moved away, as you know, with this guy whose name I'm not gonna give you, because I gotta protect myself here, too. But anyways, they went south for a bit, like honeymoon extended, to Cuba and Hawaii and everything,

for a year almost. He had some oil money. And then eventually they moved to Nova Scotia 'cause he had family there, but
they're back in St. John's now, moved back here once Alex went
to Toronto with you. I sees her every now and then, but we
don't get along the best. She's not like she used to be. Colder,
more ostentatious, more "practical," she says.

I loved how Wanda spoke mostly in loose dialect but also
with big words from books. She knew more words than anyone
I knew, probably.

Did you tell Alex where she was? I asked.

No, my dear. He was stayin' with me, so I was right caught
up in between it all for a while there. She was all, like, pissed
about that with me, but I said to her, I said, Rosey, what the
hell am I supposed to do, send him out in the streets? So it was
okay, he's such a sweet boy, like his father more than anything.
And she's stay-at-home with the kids —

She has kids, I said, feeling my face get hot. I imagined Alex
getting news like that, the whiplash of having to catch up to it, like
all of the ideas he formed about her getting away, dissolving, and
rewriting themselves into his past — it's different, getting away
from family altogether versus getting away to start a new one.

She's got two young ones, yeah, said Wanda, barely noticing
me anymore, the whiskey giving her the sheen of a respected ora-
tor with a rapt audience. Anyways, I didn't really know what he
was up to, said he was just gonna visit some friends and whatnot,
but then one day I comes home from work and a bunch of my
address books and notebooks and things are all opened on the
table, and Alex is gone, and sure enough her information was all
up in there, and my laptop password is just Wanda. So anyways,
sure enough he figured it out before he battered to fuck.

When was that? I asked.

Just a couple of days ago, she said. So Rosey won't talk to me now, thinks it's my fault. And then Robert calls, and now here *you* are, and to be honest it's all got me drove, drove ta drink, but at least it's a bit of excitement, I s'pose. You know, things get pretty dull here after a while, and I'm not cute like I used to be.

I spent the next hour or so telling Wanda that she was a hot commodity, that she should come to Toronto for a visit, where she could get some "real dick," as she called it. I got the bill while she was gone to the bathroom and told her I'd call her again if I stuck around for much longer, though the whole time from when she told me about Alex's mom on, I couldn't really focus at all, and all of the feelings I had had through the day, the acute pangs of concern and sadness and loneliness and nostalgia, washed away, making me numb, like everything was far away and nothing could reach me, even though of course that wasn't true at all.

When I got back up to my room, I lay down on the giant, cold bed and felt so exhausted, like I wanted to sleep for a hundred years. I looked at the time and it was 9:00 p.m. I started to drift off to sleep, in and out, and felt the threat of the Old Hag gathering in the periphery of my subconscious, as if my brain's different modes of interpretation presented themselves like the pages of a book, each page a flat and thin layer of consciousness, and the book was falling and you didn't know which page it would open to when it landed, but she — the Old Hag — was on some of those pages, waiting to jump out of the page and take over whoever looked at it. It felt something like that but was weirder, and more psychedelic, and harder to explain.

It felt like I was falling in and out of sleep for hours, but when I opened my eyes it was only 9:45, and something in me remembered I had a plan. I wanted to find Alex, but not to-night. I would find him in the morning, when emotions were running less high and the fog wasn't so thick, covering the whole moon. The daytime seemed better, the daytime when everyone was sober and showered and new.

But then I remembered: Bobby! The Facebook convo we had had seemed like weeks ago, but I was supposed to go to his house tonight in the outfit I wore to Robert Delaney's house, and we were supposed to have sex and be together, and a little cocoon of comfort and the past and present and future was there waiting for me, a bright spot. It seemed impossible to imagine, but it wasn't impossible; it was real and it was true and I felt like I loved him for it.

I jumped out of bed, had the fastest, coldest shower, put on the nightie and knee-high socks and the jacket, smeared purple lipstick onto my eyelids and lips like how Maggie taught me, and put a bit of product in my hair, making it fall nicely with a bit of curl. I looked pretty good and always felt hotter in Newfoundland anyways, like my sort of wholesome and round face was considered more beautiful here, more familiar and welcoming, though I wasn't feeling very welcomed overall.

I walked as fast as I could down Water Street toward the Battery, that area of St. John's that comes up when you goo-gle Newfoundland on Google Images because it's so idyllic and specific. From the other side of the harbour, it looked incredible and otherworldly — water, and then all of these little bright-coloured houses perched as if cascading down the side of the cliff and surrounded by rock and green. The Battery was right next to downtown St. John's, but the second you started walk-ing up the steep and narrow road toward the top of it, it felt like you were in a different world altogether, outside of time and far from any city. It started to rain, the fog cold and gathering, and as I descended the steps into the thick of the mountain's edge, I felt myself shiver. I could picture Bobby then, as I had seen him years ago when I went to his tiny little rickety house that felt like it could topple over at any moment, and inside it was filled with the warmth of the wood stove and the smells of gingerbread or beans or stew. I decided not to think of the bad things, like how often he would ignore me when I came in the door ready to embrace him, unable to stop tinkering with whatever he was doing. Instead I thought about the good times, or, if there weren't any that I could really remember, I filled them in and scrapbooked together images and flashes of that period of life, us climbing the hill to pick blueberries on Signal Hill or sleeping outside his house under the stars.

But when I knocked on his door like he asked me to, at exactly 10 p.m., it wasn't Bobby who answered at all. Instead it was a woman I had known a little bit, Jessie, who Alex had hooked up with that night on Halloween so many years ago, Jessie with long blond hair and big blue eyes and round cheeks like mine.

We were sort of like bizarro versions of each other, actually, like sisters with slightly different interests. At least on the surface; I didn't really know her.

I was about to say hello and ask if Bobby was home when she came at me in her bathrobe like a really big enraged bird, flying toward me and yelling, calling me a whore and a bitch and a stupid fucking little slut. Then she pushed me back out of the door, and I fell down the step I had been standing on, onto the wet interlocking brick of the road below, the back of my long coat catching on a rosebush so that the coat opened and revealed what I was wearing underneath.

I sat there looking up at her, feeling shocked and defensive. She looked a little sorry for a moment and then enraged again. What the hell was her problem, anyways?

Then I remembered Ashley and Janette earlier, how they had been Jessie's best friends back in the day.

Then I remembered seeing pictures of Jessie on Bobby's Facebook and her pictures of him posted to her Instagram.

And *then* I remembered one picture I had seen that she had posted, which I hadn't thought about in a long time but that had struck me at the time, about a year before: the inside of Bobby's little cabin, similar to how it used to be, little wool blankets, and an old tape player, map on the wall. But in the picture *her* things were in there, too, her touch. Pink thrifted curtains and pillows, patches pinned to the wall from girl pop punk bands like Hop Along and Old and Weird.

Suddenly it all made sense. Bobby was with Jessie. He had been the whole time.

Before I got the chance to explain anything, though, she spat down at me and started talking.

You little bitch, now that you're on the mainland you think you can just come back and fuck whoever you want, well, let me tell you something. I *saw* your messages! Bobby said you *threw* yourself at him and that even after he resisted, you sent him that fucked up message about all the times you've ever *had* *sex*, like a fucking *crazy* person! I screenshotted it and sent it to pretty much everyone, so now everyone knows you're a crazy little entitled brat with zero fucking integrity.

I remembered how Jessie had liked Alex so much, too, back in the day. But Alex hadn't felt the same way, and then she always rolled her eyes when she saw us together. I got up, wiped the spit off my shoulder where it had landed and tried to look

Jessie in the eye. Behind her, I saw Bobby with his back to us in the kitchen, like nothing was even going on.

Then one of their indoor cats, Mist, got out and started to run away.

It didn't seem like Jessie could get more pissed, but that did it. I felt like I was watching her in slow motion, like I was a dumb baby waiting for someone to pick me up. I couldn't think of anything to say — it seemed like too much to explain, and she wouldn't believe me.

I tried to climb the side of the hill that Mist escaped up in a meagre attempt to get her back. It wasn't fair for Jessie to be in a relationship with such a lying, narcissistic piece of work and also lose her cat, too, because of it. But when she saw me trying to help she exploded into a fit of rage as yet unprecedented and started screaming.

GET THE FUCK OUT OF HERE BEFORE I FUCKING SLICE YOUR THROAT YOU BITCH, she yelled.

Something in her eyes in that moment, I knew she probably really would. She probably really would slice my throat. I started to quickly walk away, feeling terrible. I'm so sorry, I whispered to Jessie, though she couldn't hear me.

I thought of Bobby sitting quietly in the kitchen while this was going down, how he didn't get up to help find Mist even though, of course, he could hear everything that was happening. It probably wasn't her fault that she was so full of rage, I thought. Bobby was a really terrible boyfriend, his presence cold and wrong. I had been sugar-coating it with wishful thinking, taking the blame. But then I saw that it was really true: I had left Bobby because he really *wasn't* there when my mom died. He really didn't rise to the occasion at all.

I remembered the day of her funeral, a day I had long pushed into the deepest recesses of my memory house. I tried to remember him at the funeral, standing beside me.

But he wasn't there at all; he had a band practice that day. Alex was right — Bobby really was the worst.

And I hadn't really been in a long-term relationship since.

Then it dawned on me. I didn't just hide my heart because I was heartbroken over my mom, a reality that would never change or fix itself.

I had also learned to hide my heart because of Bobby.

I started walking away from the house and farther out toward the tip of the Battery, past the occupied houses and toward some old abandoned ones that Alex and I used to hang out in. It was windy and cold and raining but it didn't really matter, even though I wasn't sure why I was going there.

I knew I should have felt even worse after all of that, that it would have been nice to catch a break and be in someone's arms and have amazing sex. Before seeing the reality of Bobby's situation, it felt like that was the only thing I could have wanted, the only thing that would have made anything feel better.

But leaving, I felt like some cavern within me that had felt dark and impossible to enter for so long was now being lit upon, and now I could really look at it. Maggie had always made me feel homesick for a place that I couldn't remember, but maybe that place was inside of me, or between Maggie, Alex, and me, or upheld in the memory of my mother, something raw and strange that existed in a feeling that could only occur when you really love someone, and with that feeling I watched the moon softly drift under the clouds, appearing as a blip of warmth and light before disappearing again and again, always there but mostly hidden. Bobby had hurt me, had had an effect that tangled itself with the eclipsing feeling of losing my mother, and I had been enveloped in all of it so it felt like a ball of hurt wrapped itself around me, as if all of the pain was the same, and if I couldn't move through some of it, then that meant that I couldn't move through any of it.

It was true, there was some pain, grief, loss that felt really impossible to overcome, pain that could only be tucked away for moments long enough to eat or breathe or sleep or laugh, pain that had no answer.

But then there was other pain that I could move through, a different kind altogether.

There was a bottle of wine that I had stolen from my dad's house, Jackson Triggs Merlot, and I knew he'd never drink it. I had put it in my backpack, and I had forgotten but then remembered it walking down the hill as I heard Jessie's voice, calling out to Mist in the distance, fading behind me. I wasn't drunk anymore and actually felt more sober than I had in a long time, like the clarity in my mind rang with such intention that it woke parts of me up I didn't know existed. I felt guilty, but newly alert and capable.

At the far point of the Battery where I was heading, the point the farthest out in the harbour, the last stop, I gazed at the two abandoned houses that I used to hang out in with Alex. They were both saltbox houses built on planks over the water, remarkable for the fact that they basically appeared as houses that were more or less in the water itself, elevated above it, but when the tide went up and the wind made waves, it almost looked like those two houses were really floating on the water like Jesus. I couldn't figure out how they hadn't fallen down and how the water hadn't made the wood rot away, but I guessed there was cement below the wood, or something to keep them up. Either way, they were barely standing at this point, and getting into either of them would be really hard: To get into the closest one, you had to take a loose, rotting two-by-four and throw it toward the crumbling front deck of the house, the gap between the ground and the deck about ten feet deep, just crumbling rocks and water below, and three or four feet across. The other house was basically impossible to get into, but if you really wanted to, you could take another piece of wood and create a plank between both houses, though if you fell off of that plank it would probably be the last thing you ever did.

I felt okay just sitting on the hill and looking out at the water, drinking the wine, and shifting between intermittent moments of feeling in awe of nature and of looking at my phone.

I looked at Facebook and saw that Bobby had, in fact, sent some follow-up messages in the past hour that I hadn't seen. They were polite and calculated and clearly full of lies, stuff about how he and Jessie had been broken up when we slept together, but he had come home and they had gotten back together, and she had felt uneasy about his time away and had snooped through his things, finding the messages between us. He tried to play her off as "intense" and "jealous" because she had snooped, but I doubted they had been broken up really, since they clearly still lived together, and her cat was there and everything. There's a thing people talk about in Newfoundland, being voted off the island. Like if you really fuck up or a rumour is spread about you in St. John's, you're not allowed to come back. You have to go, and everyone rallies together to make sure you can't get away with it.

No one would ever rally against Bobby. He was sexy and had accomplished many projects. I had already left, so I was an easy sacrifice. It would be way easier for everyone to hate

me than for them to come to terms with the facts of Bobby. I
didn't really blame anyone for it; it was an island mentality that
I remembered, one where there aren't that many resources and
so new things that threaten the foundation feel like intrusions.
It felt helpless and wrong that he could go around and just do
whatever he wanted forever and never have to face himself,
but that wasn't really my problem anymore, plus no one really
believed in fairness these days.

The longer I sat there, the more and more inviting the abandoned house became. It looked really lonely, and I had the urge
to light it up, just a little, just for a minute.

The first time I had gone into the house was with Alex when
we were nineteen and had just moved to St. John's. We lived
in residence up at the university, but one of the first weekends
after we had moved to the city from Corner Brook, we decided
to go downtown. I remember feeling like a grown up for the
first time, like everything new that I was seeing and experiencing had intention, was weaving itself into some imagined
future that was whole and perfect and had a set point of destination. Alex had a tape player with classical tapes his dad had
given him, and we brought chips and beer and a blanket and a
flashlight with us, not really knowing where we were going or
what we would do once we got there.

We walked until the sun started to set and then came upon
the two houses. Without talking about it, Alex started to con-
struct little planks so that we could walk over the gap between
the land and the house's door and get inside. Once we were in
there, I was really surprised to see that the inside of the house

still looked sort of lived in — there was furniture, and water-logged books on the floor, and beer bottles, and even a deck of cards splayed about the room like someone had decided to play 52 pickup, the worst card game. It looked like someone had lived there fifty years before and had just gotten up and left one day, and the house was trying to wait for that person to return, was trying to keep itself cute and intact, which was relatable.

I started tearing at the wallpaper, which was split and swollen in many places like a busted lip. The best time of life, maybe, is when you just start to stop being a child, because you spread the child sheen onto adulthood, and so everything feels playful and bright but also important. I felt sexy like a pop star walking through the house and touching things, as if Alex was watching me touch the room around me and was admiring the movements that my limbs made as they cut through the air.

It felt like *we* were important, like we were really *living* and not just thinking about living, which was what we had done as children, really. Like we were living in a safe bubble but that bubble was expansive, could grow in the air, and envelop more and more of life into it. Alex seemed to be feeling that way, too. That exact way. He looked at me and I knew he was.

We had sex for the first time then on his blanket. Not just the first time with each other, but it was the first time for either of us, ever. It was cold and the floor hurt my knees. I got on top of him, and it seemed like the floor might cave in below us. If it did, it might have washed us both out to sea. We took our pants off but left our jackets on. It didn't feel how I thought it would feel. He held my hips and bit his bottom lip in concentration, his long pale body, musical limbs, the way his hair came down over one shoulder as he lay down on the scratchy red blanket, the shock of him going inside me, good pain.

It didn't last very long. He pulled out of me in a panic and came all over the blanket, and we both started laughing hysterically, though I was also crying a little. Some sort of fuzzy classical music was playing in the background from his tape player, and I had the thought only after that maybe he had planned it, even though the energy that presented itself between us felt different from anything that happened before that, and it didn't really remain that way afterward either, and it didn't really make a Big Feeling grow in some sort of predictable way. Having sex didn't make us fall in love in the way that people say that two people might fall in love when they take each other's virginity or make love generally, even though we were already in love in our own way.

We left the dirty blanket there, and the next time we went back the blanket was gone, which we both found so funny, the idea that some random person might have that blanket on their couch now and they have no idea.

After we had sex, we just lay there, drinking beers and eating chips, my head on Alex's stomach, him propped up half on his elbows in a way that seemed uncomfortable but he said wasn't. It felt like we were inside of a snow globe, the dust floating around us like sparkling little particles of magic.

When we left I felt so calm for the whole walk, and the next day things felt more or less as they had before we had sex, and we didn't do it again for a long time. I thought that having sex with Alex would fill me and quell the Big Feeling inside, flooding the vast interior to its brink, quieting whatever voice was yelling out in there, whatever voice echoed through the chambers of my nothingness. I thought that, maybe, having sex with Alex would be like reaching the boss in Mario, where Alex and the Big Feeling face off once and for all, and some child part of me had been waiting for that all of the years since I first felt it.

It made me feel silly and sleepy and nice and coy and sweet, having sex with Alex. It made me feel loved. But having sex with Alex didn't make me feel the Big Feeling at all, not like the idea of it did.

Climbing into the house this time was a lot harder than before, because I was tipsy and alone, and because of the rain, and because more of the wood had swollen and disappeared with the weather. I found a good plank and threw it toward the deck of the house, but when I bent over to try and push its far end farther onto the deck, I overshot and slipped on the grass, nearly falling to the rocky sharp expanse below where waves crashed and lapped up toward me. I managed to get across and shimmy my way in through the broken door, careful about the rusty nails I could feel scratching my jacket from the outside as I slid through.

Once inside, I couldn't help but think about all of the waiting in life. There was Maggie, waiting for a baby and for Alex and for me, and there was Robert Delaney, waiting for his love, who would never come back because she was entirely different now and had rewritten herself. There was Jessie, waiting for Bobby to be a good man, or maybe she wasn't waiting for that at all. Had my mother been waiting? Had she been waiting for life to turn itself over and reveal something new? She had so many friends and things she liked to do, planting tulip bulbs, taking long walks around the lake, knitting, watching television shows, so much reading. She had me and I had her.

Maybe her vast interior held relics that I could never imagine, pieces that existed outside of language. Just as our moods do not remember each other, there is no way for us to remember or to really know the moods of others or what they reveal.

The wind caterwauled through the cracks in the house, and I got up to look out to the water. Through the window I looked at the other house adjacent to this one, the one that was harder to access and smaller. I saw a flicker of light in there that went as soon as it appeared. The flicker startled me, but I thought that it was probably in my mind, until a few seconds later the orange light bloomed up again and died down to a tiny red dot. Fear danced through my neck and back — maybe it was the Old Hag, or maybe there were people squatting here, like I knew there had been before.

I went onto the tiny back porch and saw that a plank had been set between both houses. I reached my body over the railing to get a better look inside the other window, but it was dark and the glass was dirty.

Then I saw his face. It was Alex.

I went inside and quietly sat down facing him, leaning my forehead into his. He didn't talk for a while, just leaned back, laughed, and wrinkled his brow in a way that revealed deep annoyance and relief at once. I thought I would feel calmed to find him, but once we were face to face, I didn't really know what to say or where to start, so I lay down on his stomach, and gave him the rest of my wine, even though he was clearly already sort of drunk.

We sat there for a long time until I almost fell asleep and got really cold. I felt him shuffle around, and when I opened my eyes I saw him rubbing his face with both his hands.

Mom gave me thirty thousand dollars, he said finally.

I thought about this for a minute.

Wow, I said.

So I guess it's like I really *did* go tree planting.

It's not, though.

No, he said, it's not.

There was another long pause, and I watched the moon appear, just the edge of it, just for a moment, between thick sheets of fog over the harbour.

Wanda said that Prowler is playing at The Ship tonight. Do you want to go? I asked, and Alex started laughing. Then we both sat up and he put his arm around me in an exaggerated way, like a dad on a sitcom.

All right kids, settle down, he said.

Okay, Dad, I said, feeling him stiffen with the title.

We're old now, he responded in a radio voice. And things are straaaange.

Did you take the money?

Yeah, it was deposited directly into my bank account.

What was it like to see her?

She sort of acted like we were in a job interview. She asked me if I had any questions. I don't know, it was weird. She had these two kids hanging off her, so she was distracted, I guess.

He tried to say this without emotion, but I could hear how hard he was trying to sound that way, flattening his voice out along a plane.

Did you ask her anything? I asked.

Nah, he said. I asked her what time it was.

Nice.

Ha, yeah.

Did the kids look like you?

A bit, yeah, but chubby.

Cute.

Alex shook his head, and then he sighed heavily and started to whistle. Then, mid-melody, he spoke with urgency.

I wondered if we were alike, but it didn't really feel like there was anything between us, like we couldn't really understand each other's context. I felt sort of like I was talking to a ghost.

You're not like her at all, I said to him, but he didn't respond or make a noise.

I was worried about you, I said.

I was worried about you, but I wasn't that worried. Because seeing her must have taken a lot of bravery, but you *are* brave, so ...

I trailed off. He didn't want compliments, because he didn't want to exist too much, not in that moment.

I had sex with your dad. He's hot, I said instead.

Get the fuck out of here, yelled Alex, laughing, pushing me slowly by the shoulder, where I rolled sideways onto the floor and started to laugh.

I'm not going anywhere, I responded.

By the time Alex came back, Maggie was showing a little, though she said it was probably all of the chips. Ketchup chips.

I used to find them disgusting, but now they're my favourite thing, she said.

I was calling the baby Babybel by that point, after those little cheese wheels in the red wax, and Maggie was calling it Pony and sometimes Lobsterman, after the sunburnt guy in the reality television show we had been watching.

We moved into a bigger apartment in the Junction that one of Alex's film "friends" had left behind when he moved to Berlin. It was a good deal, a real stroke of luck, rent-stabilized and two floors and only two thousand dollars a month, which was good for Toronto. It was charming and sort of dirty and old, with a brown oven and windows that were painted shut. It wasn't really practical, but it was full of charm and promise. The top floor, where I lived, was more of a self-contained attic apartment, with a pitched roof and a small kitchenette, though there was a real kitchen and living room downstairs. Babybel's room was to be in the smaller office room. As soon as we moved in, I started replacing panes of glass in all of the rooms with stained glass, so that the light would bleed into the apartment in beautiful ways, and Maggie took to painting the walls of Babybel's room, all of the faces of everyone she had ever met, in light yellow paint.

The faces were scary and detailed, with eyes too big and tiny mouths and lines like wrinkles.

I told Maggie that I thought the faces would be scary for Babybel, but she said that they would be good, because she wanted the baby to know that there were so many people out there, and if they looked at all of those faces, they would never feel too alone in the world. I installed a light pink glass window over Babybel's window, and the pink light shimmered and danced against the wall like the light from an indoor swimming pool.

There was a photo from the album at my dad's house that I took back to Toronto with me that I decided I would frame and put in the window of my cute new room, which I loved, although sometimes I hit my head on the ceiling. I had forgotten taking the photo with me in the rush of leaving my dad's house; it was in one of those photo albums where the pictures adhere to a sticky white backdrop that is covered in a see-through plastic film. In the photo, I am six years old, standing next to my mother, all dolled up for my cousin Tiffany's wedding. Looking through the album, I liked the photo, because my mom is staring directly into the camera, smiling, and I'm holding her hand, looking up at her with a savage grin on my face, wide-eyed and bright. We're standing in front of the United Church on West Street on a windy summer day, and I'm holding a basket with some wildflowers in it, and my hair is in a big curly ponytail, and I'm wearing a big puffy dress covered in yellow pears, and my mom is wearing a navy pantsuit and a red scarf, and her lips are red, too.

I thought I remembered that wedding pretty clearly, because I remember crying, finding out that my cousin Tiffany had picked my other cousin, Jillian, to be the flower girl for the wedding, even though we were the same age, Jillian and I. I guess that in the end, Tiffany had liked Jillian more, and maybe they spent more time together than we had, but the choice felt like a personal blow to me at the time, because I wanted to play the part of the flower girl so badly, and it didn't seem like Jillian even cared. I had gotten in trouble at the family dinner the night before for pulling Jillian's hair when she tried on her flower girl dress, which was dark purple and had a little velvet bow at the front.

Jillian looked so lovely and perfect in the dress and said that she would be allowed to wear lipstick to the wedding because of her role, and it made me so mad that I yanked on Jillian's hair, and she screamed bloody murder and all the adults came in.

My mom sent me to a time out for the hair pulling, and I cried and cried. But then, the next morning, the morning of the wedding, on our way to the church she got Dad to pull over, and she took me to a walking trail full of power lines near our house where some wildflowers grew, a spot where we picked blueberries in late July. She said I could be a flower girl, too, that it didn't matter that Jillian was allowed to walk through the church. She said that I could bring flowers and give them to whomever I wanted. I picked the flowers, pulling them from their roots so that all of the dirt came with them, staining my hands, and I passed them around like that, bits of soil falling into people's hands as they accepted the offerings.

I took the picture back to Toronto with me because it reminded me that it's important to stay close to people who love you enough that they will let you be yourself, even in moments of ugliness or unreason, even when the rest of the world finds you to be a bit much.

In my room, the picture fell out of my notebook onto the floor face down while I was unpacking, and I picked it up.

But then I noticed on the back of the photo something I had forgotten that my mother always did, which was that she always wrote the date and time a photo was taken on its reverse side. On the back of the photo, in her slanted cursive, were the words "Sophie and I, Tiffany's wedding, 1997, United Church, West Street, 11:15 a.m."

Seeing the note filled my heart with surprise. Because in the photo, my hair is messy, and there's dirt on my face, and the flowers are all jumbled up and imperfect in their basket, whereas I remember feeling pristine, and I remember the flowers overflowing in the basket and in perfect order, even though I had known what I had pulled up with them.

Looking at the photo, I had always thought that it was taken in the aftermath of the event, and that the look on my face was one of pride and fulfillment for having done a good job as a fake flower girl.

But in real life, I was just looking at my mother with all of that love and joy because, maybe, that's how I always looked at her, and nothing had even happened yet.

Acknowledgements

THANK YOU TO MY PARENTS AND BROTHER FOR YOUR unwavering support. You've always given me votes of confidence that make the impossible feel possible and I will never stop being grateful for that. Thank you to Sheila Heti for being my brilliant mentor, thank you to Bob McGill and everyone in the U of T Creative Writing cohort, to Julie Mannell for believing in the manuscript early on, to Russell Smith, my wonderful editor, and to the rest of the Dundurn team, who are great. Thank you to ArtsNL and SSHRC for the generous grants that enabled me the time and space to write and polish this book. Thanks to Lee Suksi, Scott Sheppard, Shosh Ganz, Tim Baker, Ian McCurdy, Meghan Hollett, and all of the friends who have helped me along the way. Your encouragement, patience, and insight have meant the world.

About the Author

ALEY WATERMAN IS A THIRTY-two-year-old writer from Corner Brook, Newfoundland. After many years away in St. John's and Toronto, she is back in Corner Brook working as an English professor at Grenfell Campus, Memorial University of Newfoundland. While she misses the city, she spends lots of time in the mountains back home, and visits Toronto and Montreal often. When she's not teaching or writing, you can find Aley reading, hanging with friends, playing and recording music for one of her four bands, skiing or, if it's summer, swimming on the mountain, and making stained glass mosaics (this part of the novel was autobiographical). She has a deep infatuation with stained glass that she can't really explain. She lives with her cat Marg in a whimsical little townhouse apartment next to a haunted manor in downtown Corner Brook.

A graduate of the M.A. in creative writing from the University of Toronto, Aley worked on her first novel, *Mudflowers*, under the mentorship of Sheila Heti. Aley has had poetry, prose, and creative essays published in the *Brooklyn Review*, *Bad Nudes*, the *Hart House Review*, the *Trampoline Hall* podcast, *Newfoundland Quarterly*, *Riddle Fence*, *Vault Zine*, Metatron Press's *ÖMËGÄ*, and elsewhere. She is currently working on her second novel.